Ack

Well, here it is people, a lot of writers dream about having their first book out for sale. But I will tell you this. It is not a particularly easy path being an artist.

There is the fear of rejection, of what others may think, or a general distrust of people. A writer lets you inside their head, something most people guard with their lives.

This book is for two different types of people: First, for anybody who has completed a body of work. You sat down, wrote like hell, and stayed focused. You are a real anomaly. Be proud that you accomplished what most people wish they could.

Second, this is also for anybody chasing a dream, whatever that may be.

You're on your way, or perhaps your dream is to write a book, but you have never written anything in your life. That's all okay. Work hard, don't look back, and do not stop for anybody.

I would like to thank a handful of people.

My parents, my brother, for always believing in me and giving me the opportunity to dream. I love all of you, and I promise that this is just the beginning.

To my dearest friends and colleagues at home and across the globe. Special thanks to Juan Bruno, a true artist, for your words of encouragement. To Cody Steffick, a great friend in a dire time. To Devon Hewett, best of luck with your own writing. To the gypsy, because you are. To my 12th-grade creative writing teacher, Mr. Stephenson. The best teacher I ever had. Thank you for opening the door.

Lastly, in the memory of Bryce LaFon. Thank you for your friendship.

Insomnia Café

*A collection of stories and dark romantic poetry
to keep you up at night*

By Kyler

Side A – 11:59 pm:
One Minute Before Midnight

Side B – 12:01 am:
One Minute After Midnight

6:08 am:

The Morning After
(Poetry & other Observations)

Instruction Manual

So, you want to be a famous horror writer?
Child, put on your boots and hat.
Pack a suitcase and put on a smile.

We are going to send you away for a while.
Only the disturbed are welcome here.
We have arranged a ride for you.
Take the candy from his hand. Get in the car.

Come back with a couple of stories.

The
Stories

The Killer.

Ladies, if you hire someone to murder your husband, make sure that you get the right person for the job. It's about the money with these types of people. The Killers. My hair is done, and I had spent the better half of the afternoon trying to look presentable. I probably look better for a murderer than I ever looked for my husband of fourteen years. This is business.

I had hired a murderer to end my husband's life. The Killer asked me for his work schedule. My husband gets off work at five-ten, and he is home by six. Now it's dark outside, and the dinner I prepared is cold. My husband is always home for dinner. His absence is a good sign. There is a knock at the door, my Killer, coming to tell me the news. Is my husband dead, and did The Killer bury him six feet under? Either way, I'll have to let the sociopath into to my house to find out what happened. Let's do this.

I open the front door; The Killer is expressionless. He walks past me, looking around. "So, is it done?" I murmur. We talk in the dining room. He pulls out a chair for himself, sitting at the opposite end of the dinner table to me.

The house is quiet, like the dead. A clock on the wall ticks. The Killer sits back, pulling a long steel knife out of his jacket and puts it on the table

"I put this knife to his throat, then made him get down on both knees. He begged for his life," he says. My heart thumps. He used that on my husband. "He asked me how much you paid me. Like he knew." My face goes pale, I feel sick. "Then?" I stutter.

The Killer grins, "Well then, he offered me more." The Killer stands up, picking the knife off the table. He starts to walk towards me.

Halfway To Nowhere

Sometimes she would close both of her eyes and pretend she was dead. Instead, she adjusts the rifle on her shoulder, keeping a finger curled around the trigger. The older you get, the closer you are to death. The in-between part is called living. Or halfway to nowhere.

If the young woman pulled the trigger right now, the old woman's brains would be splattered across the walls of her home. Like scrambled eggs on a breakfast plate. The old woman had been a wife and mother but that had been a long time ago and a couple thousand miles away.

The old woman couldn't bear taking on such responsibilities of a family. So, the woman left.

The young woman lowers the rifle, setting it down beside her. The target moves away from the window, blowing black tobacco smoke up into the night sky. The rest of the evening is a colorful pigmentation of game shows or TV dinners. Until she fell asleep, pretending to play dead. Like we all do. Tomorrow would be the same, rinse, wash, repeat. But when the old woman woke up in the morning, the whole day was her creation. The target didn't believe that you could put a price on that.

While her assassin rolls over, leaving the gun in the thick foliage. She pulls out a knife from her jacket pocket, approaching the house. The deed would be done up close. Life is chalked full of bits of irony. The young woman knocks on the door, with the knife hidden behind her back. A warm tumbleweed blows across the front porch, stopping at her feet. The young woman smiles, holding out both of her arms. The old woman just stares at her face, and then at the knife. Every responsibility in her life came flooding back. There were no other choices. "Hello, mother," The young woman whispers.

The Jar

It's midnight; there is a tap on my bedroom window. An old man presses his face up against the glass. He wants to be let inside. What happens next is up to him, he tells me, smiling like a child on Christmas morning. On his neck is a black ink tattoo of an octopus. In his right hand is a knife.

The octopus is my favorite animal, do you know why he grins; a yellow crooked smile. "They are just as smart as humans. As a young man, I watched an octopus trying to get into a glass jar with a fish inside. It struggled, tossing the jar around but it would not break until frustrated, it used its tentacles to twist and pull the jar open like a human. Pop. Swallowing the fish whole".

He looks back at me with hungry eyes. I scream, shutting the blinds. The old man moves around the back of my home searching for entry points. The patio door is locked as well as the door to the garage. He couldn't get in, could he? I hope not.

I'm quick, moving from room to room. Tipping a cabinet over in front of the bedroom window. I fall to my knees, exhausted. A whisper of warm air hits the back of my neck, the kitchen window, pushed up an inch if that. Terrified, I scramble to both feet, closing it. An inch too much. I feel the edge of the knife to my throat; he's behind me. Smiling.

"The octopus will eventually find its way into the jar; it's smarter than the fish." He whispers in my ear.

The Face

Penelope told herself that one-day people would notice her. It was just a matter of being at the right place at the right time. What else did she have besides her delicate features? A life behind the camera was not worth living.

Last week Penelope had taken a small hammer and shattered all the mirrors in her tiny apartment, cackling like a roguish hyena. She would empty the bits of glass into a wastebasket and then place it into the bin, outside. She wouldn't be reminded of her flaws when brushing her teeth or doing something so rudimentary. Penelope knew she had a lot to acquire, and a defeatist attitude was not the answer in Hollywood. Her looks would give her a career, and eventually, within time, an identity with the public. But most important of all life.

She had already started taking acting lessons. Penelope was going to become world famous for her aesthetics. Little girls would watch her on the television and look up to her; they just didn't know it yet. Her looks would make her a matinee idol, at least in her own mind. The public opinion would vary.

By the industry standards, she had it all. The woman had big round beautiful eyes, a broad pearly white smile, and clear porcelain skin hung up on a rack in her room. The two eyes were floating in a glass jar, next to another jar with a pair of ears. She had cut them off a gorgeous face and kept her aesthetics in separate jars for herself. The bloody knife that she had used had been cleaned and put back in the dishwasher.

Penelope spent the better half of the morning with a sewing thread and needle. Stitching together the ears, two eyes, the sharp nose, and plump red lips onto a fleshy mesh of rubber, and matted hair. When she is done, she tugs the rubber mask down over her head.

She begins to cry, clapping her hands together. Gorgeous.

For A Better Tomorrow

A typical lesson with your hand-made wood tipped spears is to keep them pointed away from your body, even when held above your head and drumming the air like a native savage.

He plunges his spear into the water. When he pulls the spear out of the water, two fish are impaled on the sharp tip of the spear together in a passionate kiss.

Together the man and the young woman would eat the fish using the spears as large kabob skewers.

He fucks his wife on the beach. He fucks her harder and faster than ever before. They fall asleep together, next to an orange campfire on the beach. Both of their appetites fulfilled.

Some people will not be controlled by a decaying society. The couple left for a better tomorrow. It was easy after the two found the island. It was their paradise, or so they thought.

Further on down the beach, a red, bright firefly dances in a glass bottle next to a campfire. The beautiful woman gyrates her hips, moving them back and forth. Dancing on into the night. The beautiful woman was much the same. She had abandoned a lonely and unforgiving society for something much better.

The couple and the beautiful woman had agreed to share the island. They drew a line in the sand. She had one half, and they had the other.

The young woman was confident that the three of them could live together. Just as long as her husband would stop talking about the beautiful woman all the time. She could see that he was obsessed with her. She would roll over, and her husband would be up and watching the other woman dance around the fire.

The young woman knew that her husband did not love her anymore. She had lost him to another woman. It was only a matter of time till he left.

One night, she opens both of her eyes. Her husband was packing his bags. "Where are you going," The young woman stutters. Her husband does not look at her but just walks past her.

"I'm going over there," He whispers.

The young woman nods her head, understanding. "Just one last kiss, darling" She moans. Her husband nods his head, bending over to give her a peck on the cheek. The young woman grips the rock in her hand, bringing it up above his head. Before smashing it down across his face.

Far off along down the beach, the beautiful woman continues to dance, moving her hips in a slow circle. She stops, squinting both of her eyes. Somebody was coming across to her camp, moving through the dark swirling mist of the midnight hour.

It was he; she was sure of it. She feels an electric rush of electricity run through her groin. The beautiful woman begins to move forward towards him, further away from the orange campfire and into the dark. The beautiful woman runs up to her new lover, wrapping both of her arms around him. "I knew you would come for me--," The woman whispers, flicking her tongue in his ear. She runs her hand across a pair....of round breasts...

Her lover takes another step forward, revealing itself to be the face of a woman. Half of her face caked with blood. Both of her nostrils flaring and her chest beating up and down like an African drum.

The scorned woman smiles cruelly, bringing the spear out from behind her back.

Nothing Lasts Forever

He pretended to kill people for a living. That was the way he saw it. The finger that pulls the trigger and delivers the bullet is the murderer. Alistair Noble liked to call it a conditioned reflex. If you paid him enough money, he was not responsible for what happened.

Alistair carried the rifle in a violin case. He carried the violin case everywhere he went. On paper, he was an instructor and taught at an all-boys college. That was the cover. The school tended to change depending on his location.

Alistair was one of the best killers in the world. He knew that he couldn't prove it, but he and the department both knew it.

But there was a catch, you see.

Technically, Mr. Noble didn't exist. Two people knew who Alistair Noble was. One of them slept in his bed, and the other slept across the hall in a racecar bed.

Alistair was a loving husband and father. The two of them reminded him that he was human. That he was able to care about something other than the job. If you get to know a killer, you'll find out what makes them tick. Underneath flesh and blood, there is a beating heart.

That all sounds great on paper doesn't it.

But it was a great lie. It was a life that many in his profession envied. Of course, Alistair knew the truth that nothing ever lasts forever. Eventually, you'll get caught. The end to the lie comes in a dollar amount. Alistair knew in his head, it was just about how much they were willing to offer. Anyone would budge.

On this particular morning, Alistair goes downstairs for breakfast. He was usually up before his wife and would make them both some eggs.

On the kitchen counter is a duffel bag full of money. Attached to the bag is a note. "Time to get back to business," it reads.

He didn't have to think twice about who the targets were.

Both were upstairs, sleeping in their rooms.

Instead, he picks up the bag, opens the front door, shakes his head and leaves the bag on the front-step.

The following morning Alistair comes down for breakfast again. This morning there are two duffel bags on the counter.

He taps his foot nervously, then picks up the two bags, opens the front door, closes it, then walks upstairs and makes love to his wife.

On the third morning, there are four duffel bags. Alistair screams, tossing a pot of coffee onto the ground. It shatters everywhere. He makes two trips this time, throwing bag number one and two out onto the lawn.

He goes back upstairs, pinning his wife on her stomach. Fucking her until she screams. Alistair yells over and over, keeping his back arched and his toes curled. "I love you, I love you."

On the night of the third day, he does not sleep well at all. Tossing and turning. His wife sits up, looking him up and down. "Is everything all right baby?" She asks, running a hand across his chest.

"Yes, of course, go back to sleep darling." Alistair kisses her forehead. With one hand underneath the pillow, holding a gun with a finger on the trigger. Pointed towards her. He lets go of the gun.

"You know how much I love you and the life we have together. I wouldn't throw it away for anything." Alistair pleads, tears rolling down his face.

"Then fuck me like you did this morning every day, sweetheart." She kisses him, wrapping her arms around his neck. Alistair smiles, wiping away a tear and proceeds to go to work.

Afterward, the two-rollover exhausted. Alistair stares up at the ceiling hands behind his head.

His wife is already sound asleep with one hand on his chest. He tries not to laugh. He'd put on quite a show, hadn't he? Now she definitely trusted him. Just as the cash continues to flow. Alistair had missed his calling, he thought. He shoulda been a fucking actor.

In the morning, I'll be able to kill her; he snickers to himself. I'm so brilliant.

Alistair rolls over, whispering into his sleeping wife's ear. "That's all this is baby, one big game. But that's life, isn't it? We are headed towards the big payout; time to cash in my chips."

The assassin wondered what tomorrow morning would bring; he couldn't help but not picture a dump truck of cash. To be truthful, it kind of turned him on.

"I'll see you in the morning baby. Just one last payday." He grins, closing both of his eyes.

There are two things an assassin never forgets. The cold barrel of a gun pressed against your forehead and the last mistake. This morning, Alistair had to accept both.

He opens both of his eyes, sunlight flooding the room. He had overslept.

Alistair immediately goes for his gun; already knowing it isn't there. It was pressed against his head.

His wife sits on top of his chest, with her finger on the trigger. Arms steady and confident. In her other hand is a set of keys to the dump truck, hanging from a finger like a cat's toy.

"Just one last payday, huh, sweetheart." She pulls the trigger. Bang.

The Laughter

The unmistakable sound of a child's laughter is a joyous part of life. Just as the bird's chirp and the flowers grow in the springtime. It can be unless you live alone in the middle of nowhere with no wife or children.

I should not be hearing footsteps in the hallway either, outside my door, for who would be up at this hour. This is absolute madness. I imagine things. Whatever I am hearing is in my head.

Above the roof of my house is a patch of thick grey clouds where my thoughts belong. A couple of the children are downstairs in the kitchen, playing with the pots and pans.

I grunt, lifting myself out of bed. Damn kids.

When I get to the kitchen, I flip on the light. The room is empty. "All right, come on out" I whisper, opening a couple of cabinets.

The refrigerator turns on and begins to hum softly like an infant, sending electrical currents to the compressor. I turn around, staring at it for the longest moment, both hands on my hips. Hmm.

I open the refrigerator door, stepping back with one foot. Click. Light turns on inside the machine.

"Well, there you two are, had me worried," I mutter, sighing with relief.

There were a couple of limbs in the refrigerator. Three arms, two legs, a couple of fingers, and the end of a foot. I had wrapped the similar limbs together in a blue plastic wrap, stacking them on top of one another.

I reach into the back of the refrigerator and pull out something the shape of a soccer ball. The boy stares back at me with two big holes where two big eyes used to be. I guess that is why I took them. "You thought that I had gone crazy for a minute, huh. Gave me quite the scare." I laugh. Setting the head back in the refrigerator. Then shut the door. On the way back upstairs, I flip the light switch.

"Goodnight," I whisper. Whistling to myself.

Spiders

I touch my husbands' arm, begging him to kiss me and pull me aside and whisper in my ear that I am the most beautiful woman in the universe. He looks back at me, both of his eyes a still pool of black swamp water. Nothing is there.

"The universe is a big place," He replies.

A perfect marriage is a fantasy for me. I'd come to accept that, in our ten years together.

He only tells me he loves me through grit teeth. Our relationship is a way for him to blend in. That is all. My husband has his demons, as we all do.

After marriage, I thought I would be the witness to a birth of a new man. Today, I am finished chasing that dream. My husband uses our relationship for exploration. Our relationship is to him as the moon was for Neil Armstrong, spiking that American flag onto unclaimed territory. Staking claim to something that does not belong to him.

Our marriage is a sham.

In reality, he is the pilot. Guiding the spaceship. His job. He tells me mine is to feed him.

My husband mashes down the dinner I prepared for him. Hacking away with a steel knife and fork, juices dribbling down his chin. He burps, finishing the plate.

He wants seconds. But I haven't even started on my own plate.

I go into the kitchen, slopping a bunch of food onto his plate.

Then I kneel down, opening the cupboard underneath the sink. In the back of the cupboard is a silver spindle of web, spun by a giant black spider. I just stare at the spider for a moment.

Spiders are similar to humans. It's ironic that we are afraid of them. A spider will take its time to build a web. The spider does not have a choice; if it wants to feed itself, it must build one correctly. So, the spider becomes naturally passionate about the web.

People also have our passion projects. We will spend night and day in our relationships. But in the end, we are together for security. Not because we want to build one together.

When a spider begins to build a web, it will start with a single thread. Once the spider uses the thread, with any luck, the free end of the thread will catch onto another branch. Once the spider feels that the thread has caught something, it will loop around and attach the thread to the starting point. Once the web is completed, the spider will sit and wait for another insect to stumble into the trap.

Once my relationship with my husband began to fizzle, I would often find text messages or missed calls on his cell phone from other women. Sometimes there would be the irregular voice mail.

But here I was, in the middle of the web. I was trapped in this broken relationship my husband and I had built together.

In the cupboard under the sink, the black spider continues to build its web, crawling up alongside the silver pipe and around. In the spider's web is a wriggling bug, fighting for its life.

Caught in a trap.

I give my spider friend a smile. "Eat up friend. We both have long days ahead of us."

Stuck to the web are many tiny white eggs. I smile, using my husbands' knife to scrape off a couple dozen of the eggs. I mix them underneath the mush pile of food on his plate, whistling to myself.

I'm happy because I know a couple of things about my husband. I know that I need to regularly check his phone and I also know that he never helps around the house. Hence, the only cleaning that ever gets done is my part. Would he ever consider the possibility of scrubbing underneath the sink, probably not?

So, I'm happy to let my little friend continue with its life. But what really makes me smile is the fact that my husband is a pig. My husband mixes his food together; he eats quickly and is done with me.

Well, I'm done with him. Let's see another week go by. I'm happy to make him whatever he likes.

The People Upstairs

"Be quiet, do you hear it? There it is again." My friend breathes, touching my shoulder. Above our head, the ceiling croaks like a sick frog, sprinkling bits of sawdust onto our shoulders.

The thing upstairs is taking large footsteps.

"Nobody is supposed to be home, right?" My friend whispers.

Looking to me for some kind of sign. I shake my head.

"No," Is all I manage to reply. But I can see the look on his face.

"Except for the monster upstairs. It has a specific appetite for people that look like you. I think you're in luck." I half-laugh, covering my face with both hands.

"I'm fucking serious, stop playing around." My friend punches me on the shoulder.

"You're ridiculous. Stop being afraid of… "I retort, before being cut off.

Upstairs, above our head, a second part of the floor begins to creak and groan. Wailing like a ghost.

"There is somebody else!" My friend half-screams. I cup my hand over his mouth, urging him to be quiet. We track the pair above our head, footsteps in tandem.

"They are coming down here!" I spit. Now it is my turn to freak out.

We back into the corner of the room; huddled together in a frightened bunch. Upstairs, somebody opens the basement door. Swinging it over onto one side. A boy holding a flashlight stands in the doorway, arms shaking. A second much taller figure rests his hand on his shoulder.

"You see son, there is nothing to be afraid of. No one is going to get you." He smiles. "I had a bad dream-dad," The boy mutters. "Son, you have to learn about rational and irrational fear. Some things you should be afraid of, but not the basement." Father exclaims. The boy lowers his head.

"Besides, I'm sure the monsters would be just as afraid of you, as you are of them." Father laughs, patting his son on the back.

"Let's get some lunch." He closes the door.

I turn around, signaling with one crooked clawed finger to stay quiet. We are enveloped in blackness.

My friend wiggles his tail, exhaling a pound of air through his snout. Relaxing his shoulders slightly. "I think the humans are gone." He hisses; his long red forked tongue slithers about like a garden snake. When he smiles, I can see a row of reptilian sharp dagger teeth stained with bits of rat and whatever else scurries down here.

Face Value

Feet tied together, hands behind my back, handcuffed. How did I get here?

On the table to my left is a tin cup full of sharp tools on a silver platter. To my right a cardboard box full of human faces, big eyes, thin lips, and broad smiles. Beautiful people.

"But ugly on the inside," he whispers in my ear. My captor.

He'll take a sliver off my bottom lip, a birthday cake slice piece off my cheek.

Tell me how I use this scalpel and cut into your flesh, and you bleed red. Human. The red is your embarrassment.

Blood, sweat, and tears dribble down my cheek.

Underneath this human flesh, he peels back the layers, and I see everything that you cannot see. Underneath we are all the same.

Bandage yourself up with these white wraps, like the disfigured.

Heal.

Go out in the world again and remember, underneath we are all the same. You'd buried yourself for years beneath a false façade of rubber and flesh.

A human face is the most expensive Halloween mask you can buy.

Under the Apple Tree

I murdered my friend and buried him under the apple tree on top of the hill. I even picked a couple of the apples off the branches and put them in a bag and brought them home to my family. That night we had apple cobbler for dessert.

I sleep with a smile on my face and someone else's wife in my arms.

I took everything from him. You would be surprised what a loving wife and warm home inspire you to achieve. Some days after work, I drive past the apple tree and put on the brakes. I will get out of the car and walk up the hill and stand under the tree. I will place my left ear to the earth and whisper.

"If you can you hear me down there, continue to rot."

One afternoon, I decided to revisit my friend. When I get to the top of the hill, however, there is another person there. Leaning against the tree with an apple in his left hand.

My friend takes a bite of the apple and spits out pieces of brown dirt from his lips, like chewing tobacco. His face and clothes are covered in the grimy chocolate brown soot of the earth, and his smile is a musty yellow.
…..

My heart skips a beat or two. "Hell is hot, but Life can be just as cold," he says. I stutter, dropping to my knees.

"Oh, I was worried! This is a miracle that you are alive!"

My friend places a dirty hand on my shoulder. Shaking his head. "The most important lesson is forgiveness. Whatever happened, between you and me is in the past."

My world seems to rotate a little bit slower at this moment.

"You are the single greatest man I have ever— met." I choke, holding him tight. He looks away.

"I had to ask you for a favor. But you were at work all day, so I didn't want to bother you."

I nod my head. "Anything—my friend, I am here now, tell me."

My friend whispers. "I hoped that you wouldn't mind, but I stopped by the house today. Just to say…hello."

I step back, shifting both of my eyes from left to right. "Oh- "I stutter, biting my lip.

He looks up, grinning slightly. "I didn't think that you would mind. There's nothing wrong with another man talking to his wife, ….is there?"

I bite my lip, trotting two more steps back. Fumbling for the keys in my pocket.

"Of course not," I half laugh. He licks his lips. "Good…."

I begin to backpedal. Already halfway down the hill, running back towards the car. His voice echoes like a creature in a cave.

"Where are you going, my friend." He laughs, erupting from the pit of his belly.

I turn the keys in the ignition, pulling out onto the road again. "You better hurry." My dead friend shouts from atop the hill, continuing in his roaring laugh.

By now, my imagination had taken hold of me. I keep asking myself a simple question. What is a dead man capable of?

Did he touch her with his rotten fingers? Or, did he take her hand and give her a tour of the underworld. None of it matters, like a flower that tries to grow in the snow.

In my heart, I know that there is nothing that I could do. It takes me ten minutes to get home, with my foot pressed on the gas pedal.

"Oh, my darling let me know that you are here," I scream, going from one room to the other. Flipping over our bed, pushing cabinets onto their side. A man stuck in a delusion he helped create.

In the kitchen, there is a trail of dirt. I follow it out into the backyard. In the middle of the yard is a shovel stuck into the ground and a high mound of soil next to a hand dug crater. A half-excavated tomb.

My heart sinks to the pit of my stomach. My minds racing back and forth like a madman. All I know to do is to scream. If I could reach into my mouth and pull out my lungs, I would at that moment.

I take the shovel and begin to dig. Fast. Scooping up bucket full's of soil and twisted root. Plunging my dagger into the hole. Until my knuckles start to bleed, and my back is slick with sweat. The slower I dig, the less time she has.

"Reach for heaven, my darling. Come back to me." I grit, burrowing my way deeper into hell.

After a couple of hours, I collapse next to the hole. Breathing hard through my nostrils. I look up, taking in the fading afternoon sun through a pair of squinting eyeballs. In a little while, the moon will have had taken its place. Plunging me into nightfall. Then, she will be lost.

"You cannot fix your situation by digging yourself into a deeper hole." A familiar voice echoes.

My friend is standing in the doorway. He lifts his left leg and gives it a jig. Dirt spills out of the side of his pants leg.

I push myself up onto my two feet; wobbling back and forth on my toes. "Where is she, you bast–ard." I huff. Clutching my chest.

He grins. "You thought that I would bury her, underneath the home that I paid for. If only she were that fortunate."

I lunge, using the remaining strength in my torso to wrap my arms around him. He pushes me off, grabbing the shovel from my hands. He flips it over, thrusting the end of the handle into my stomach. I let out a massive gasp, rocking over onto my left side. Gasping and wheezing.

He kneels over, moving his head down towards my ear. His tongue is cold and sharp.

"I took her with me. We have a nice little plot together, under the apple tree. You would find her bones buried there, next to mine. If you want my life and home so desperately, you can have it. You can take it to the grave."

I shake my head back and forth; wriggling on the ground.

He brings the shovel down one more time, connecting with my knee. The rest is a dizzying haze of stars and stripes. When I open both of my eyes again, I'm looking up into the night sky.

He is up there, and I am down here, in the pit I had dug. Shoveling heaps of dirt onto my shoulders and chest and face.

My dead friend sees me open my eyes. He stops midway through, tilting the shovel so that the dirt pours across my face.

"If you can hear me down here; continue to rot."

KIDS

My friend and I decided to set up a lemonade stand outside of our neighborhood one summer afternoon. All we needed were a pair of hammers, some nails, two wooden slat boards, and a jar for the lemonade. We also required the secret ingredient.

We use a couple of sugar packets and fill up a jug full of water from the garden hose to make our lemonade, and then add the secret ingredient.

Our first couple of customers are people we know. A man in a summer sweater takes a sip of our lemonade and grins. "Taste terrific kids, what's the special ingredient?" He jibs. Giving us an elbow and a wink.

My friend and I look at each other and giggle. He even offers us a whole dollar, but we refuse. "Spread the word, "My friend says.

When the block is empty, my friend takes our big lemonade jar and goes behind a tree. He pees in the jar. I clutch my belly, dying laughing. We fill up the jar with water, add a splash of sugar, and swirl it around to mask the taste of piss.

Sometime later, we have half of the neighborhood in line for our thirst-quenching lemonade. My friend drinks two bottles of water an hour to keep the engine running.

Our mothers come and visit us. Both have smiles on their faces, and their hands are clasped together. "My little entrepreneurs!" The ladies would say together. We give each of them a hug like proud children.

At the end of the day, my friend takes the money. "It's mine, I did all of the work," he sticks his tongue out. My face turns red, and I stomp my foot. "That's not fair" I scream, trying to wrestle the money from his grip. Instead, he pushes me away. "Welcome to the business world." My friend replies, walking away.

That night I can barely sleep, tossing and turning on my mattress. A light flickers on in the hallway. The door opens slightly. I roll over, pretending to be asleep. My mother peeks her head in the room. "I'm really proud of you." She comes over and kisses me on the forehead.

When she closes the door, I kick myself out of bed and open the bedroom window. Across the street is my friend's house. I can see the light in his bedroom is still on. No doubt celebrating his new-found wealth.

I snort, huffing a stream of steam through my nostrils. Processing my next move.

"This isn't over" I mutter, closing the window.

The next day, my friend stands behind our lemonade stand, watching the tumbleweeds roll by, alone. He looks around the block, trying to spy on potential customers. His bladder is full and ready for business.

Off in the distance, he hears the sound of two tiny tin wheels scraping across the ground. It sounded like scratches on a record player.

He sees another boy pulling a small wagon up a long driveway. My friend continues to frown when he sees that it is me. He dashes over, keeping a good distance between himself and the wagon.

I look over at my friend and smile, offering him a plastic wrapped brownie from a small pile in my wagon. My friend takes a brownie and tosses it into the street. Then looks me over from head to toe and laughs.

I am wearing a pair of tan shorts and a shirt that is tucked in around the waist. There is a pair of tin badges on my uniform and a paper hat on my head.

"So, you're a Boy Scout now. This is your great business plan." He chuckles. I shrug my shoulders, then dig into one of my pockets and pull out a chunk of dollar bills.

My friend stops talking and looks at the cash in my hand. His face turning slightly red.

He takes a step forward and tries to grab the dollar bills in my hand, but I take a step back, watching him pitch forward onto the grass.

I stick my tongue out and walk up to the front door. I knock a couple of times, straightening my back. Somebody opens the door. An older man with grey hair and a pair of reading glasses perched on his crooked nose smiles at me.

He sees the Boy Scouts pin and the silver tray of chocolate brownies in my hand. "Well good for you. I am always happy to give back." He replies, opening his wallet.

The older man gives me a couple dollars, then unwraps one of the brownies and takes a bite. His face lights up like a Christmas tree.

"Boy, you have to tell me the special ingredient, these are delicious!" He exclaims, finishing the rest of the brownie in one bite.

My friend comes right up behind me and takes another brownie, unwrapping the soft saran wrap with a couple of fingers. He sniffs the chocolate treat and then looks up at me with wide eyes.

I smile at the old man, blushing like an adorable child. "Well, then it wouldn't be special, sir." I giggle.

Dean

Dean sits in the back of our class with a packet of Ticonderoga pencils on his desk. He would break the pencils into three tiny pieces. Then Dean would push the end tip with the pencil lead into the pencil sharpener, grinding it down until the tip was as sharp as a mini-spearhead. Half an inch in length. He would do these four times during class, or every fifteen minutes. Four little spearheads in total.

Nobody seemed to notice, except me. The rest of our homeroom class would continue to stay busy. Our teacher, Mrs. Kitchens, gets up out of her chair and walks around the class. Dean takes a piece of gum out of his mouth, sticking the mini spearheads into the gum. He looks at the empty chair.

I rub both of my palms together, smoothing out my skirt over my knees. Dean is quick, then back in his seat. My heart beats in my chest like a ticking time bomb. Mrs. Kitchens walks back to her desk. I could have said something but, I didn't. Mrs. Kitchens falls out of her chair, kicking and screaming. Loud.

Everybody in the class practically jumps out of their seats. Louder.

One of the spearheads had pushed itself up into her thigh. All the way in. Blood pouring all the way out.

After school, everybody on the bus is debating on how long it took for the ambulance to arrive. I take a seat in the back of the bus and try to tune out any conversation.

"Do you mind if I sit here?" Dean smiles, plopping down next to me.

My heart thumps. "Sure…" I mutter. "Cool," he says.

After a minute or so, he looks around. "I know you saw me, it's okay though. I picked you. I was hoping you would. I also do other crazy stuff." He unzips his backpack halfway, telling me to look inside. There was a ton of chocolate bars. "I stole them from one of cafeteria vending machines. I was thinking of feeding them to a couple of dogs in my neighborhood,"

My face is pale. I mutter, "Why."

He leans in close, grinning. "I wanted someone to know what I'm capable of."

High School Reunion Poem

Upside down smile at my high school reunion

Autonomous government at heart

Wolf among the Pigs, I grew up with sharp teeth

The dagger in my coat pocket

Plunge the blade into their hide and remove letterman jacket

Dump the beer over their head like it's game-day Friday

Slit the throats of the once popular and become famous

The Party Monster

"Let me tell you a secret. If you pour some drain cleaner into a red solo cup and mix it with some red dye, it looks an awful lot like a drink you would carry around at a house party", Sarah snickers to herself, swirling the cup of punch around in her hand.

Downstairs, the music is blaring loud, amidst a spontaneous combustion of conversation.

The party is in full swing.

He laughs, looking at me.

I wouldn't lie to you, there may have been some cruel flirting. You can tell by the way someone is sizing you up, or running their eyes up and down your body, like a scanner. Sarah knew the type.

"That sounds like something from a Stephen King novel, absolutely terrifying." He smirks. She wiggles a finger. "No, no. King is notorious for his bad endings, he wouldn't be able to get away with it," He shakes his head. "Well, look at you, my little book ner—," Sarah interrupts. "Lit major, to be exact." He laughs again.

"So, let's say you poison somebody, at this party. How would you get away with it, miss fiction?"

He grabs her red solo cup, bringing it to his lips. She smacks him on the arm, playfully. "Don't drink it silly, remember the liquor is poison!" He puts the cup down. Crossing both arms. "Tell me," He says.

She points at the cup. "I wonder whose fingerprints they would find all over the cup, now!" He stops, grinning like a shark.

Sarah takes the bottom of her shirt, wiping the rim of the red solo cup. "If this is the only part of the cup I touched, then I'm home free. I leave the cup here, and later somebody drunk at the party picks it up.

That is what makes the murder spectacular. It would be totally random.

If I were the killer, I would do it just for the satisfaction of taking another life. Nothing is pre-meditated or pre-planned. Nobody could trace me back to the victim either; it's a perfect crime. So..wal-ah. I was never here. In fact, if I did want to make entirely sure, I would give you a fake name. It will also be perfect if I don't even go to this school. Totally random. You're the fall guy." Sarah replies.

The boy laughs again, putting the cup aside. "That's pretty fucked up. What's your name, Lit Major?"

Sarah brushes a hand through her hair, acting shy? "Megan," She smirks, tracing her foot in a semi-circle.

"Well Megan, there's a beer pong table with our name on it downstairs, if you're up to it." She nods. He takes her hand, and the two head downstairs.

The red solo cup sits by itself, left alone, on the edge of the balcony.

Hands Off the Wheel

Dr. Jeffrey Joyner pulls the car up into the long gravel driveway with a secure grip on the wheel. The kind of hold a world-renowned neurosurgeon is acquired to have. Steady hands, and focus.

The home that he shared with his wife was beautiful. Encompassing four spacious bedrooms, three luxurious bathrooms, and a stylish kitchen and dining room. Their home was seclusion from the worries of the real world, and of poverty and middle-class.

Here the successful surgeon dined with top businessmen and celebrities and negotiated multi-million-dollar deals. It was the ideal lifestyle. A shy, socially misfit miscast, life couldn't have been more difficult for the young man. Friday nights were spent alone, huddled under a thick blanket with a thick textbook.

After university, he had bigger dreams than most of his peers. He had his instruments for success. Two beautiful hands. His beauties. On the operating table, he was an artist who drew life. The patient was the canvas. A masterpiece was a must. Welcome to the real world.

When Joyner eventually became successful, he made time to enjoy it. Lapping it up with the rich and elite. At last, he was famous. The nerd that got picked on and degraded was gone in a flash of smoke.

He had also married the woman of his dreams. She was stunning and gorgeous in every way. Big tits, nice ass, and a penchant for gathering another person's attention.

It wasn't odd to find Joyner peering through his old high school yearbooks, snickering to himself. Crossing out X's over whoever had done him wrong. "I win," He would mutter under his breath.

His life was in his control, or so he thought. That was in the beginning.

Dr. Joyner unlocks the front door with a spare key. Upstairs, in the master bedroom, his wife is beneath the covers; sound asleep. He had wished she were dead.

Women were an alien species. He rarely understood them or knew how to communicate with them, despite his accomplishments. But he could smell the affair on her clothes and on her things, that he bought for her. He knew that at least. He felt cheated.

Joyner had hired a private detective to track his wife and the young man that she was having an affair with. He had the photos to prove it. But she had something he wasn't prepared for, a better lawyer.

"I'm supposed to sit at the popular table now and fuck the cheerleader, but you were with someone else instead of me," He thought. He had earned her. He would end her.

He felt like a loser again, studying underneath the covers. His wife had taken everything he had earned in the divorce settlement. Including the house, and his beautiful cars. So, he would take something from her. Something she couldn't get back.

Joyner kicks down the bedroom door with a wicked grin plastered across his face.

His wife sits up, with pregnant and frightened eyes, looking at the knife in his hand.

Before she can scream, he has the knife at her throat, pushing it through the back of her head. He drops the murder weapon. Clang. His wife falls back, scratching at the hole in her throat. In less than a second, she is dead.

Joyner stares at the bloody woman on the bed, red in the face. He holds up a pair of beautiful hands in the air, covered in someone else's blood. From now on it would be just them two. He didn't need this woman or anybody else for that matter.

He had both hands.

Joyner looks down at his work. Her body is on the floor. Feeling satisfied. He could hear people cheering for him up in the bleachers. Sounding off his name. Pumping their fists in the air.

Life is good when you're popular.

"My beauties," he whispers, licking the blood off his fingers.

Dreaming
Differently

The old man rolls over, pulling the sheet up to his neck. The room is cold and black, and he cannot sleep, either. "If I fall asleep I might never wake up," he reminds himself. Every night, he lies still; the old man waits for the orange sunrise. When it comes, the old man checks another tally on a piece of paper. "Another day, another dollar," he used to tell his children.

The old man lived most of his life that way, working voraciously. Saving and barely spending till his pockets began to overflow. A recluse and a selfish husband and father, his three wives, could attest to that.

"What have I done," he cries, sickly and old, remorse of a wasted youth and a bitter end. "Here I lie on my deathbed, an old man who clings to the last drops of life. Too afraid to live, too scared to die". The old man mutters. He had lived a life in limbo.

The old man drops his head and begins to cry. "Will you keep it down, some of us are trying to sleep." Somebody replies.

The old man rolls over, looking over at the other body on top of the table. It also lies underneath a sheet with an identical toe tag around his ankle.

The body peeps its' head out from beneath the sheet, frowning. "Every single night with you, it's the end give it a rest." The body rolls back over, huffing like a child.

The old man begins to cry, lowering his head. In the mortuary the dead dream of a beautiful afterlife while the old man cannot. He starts to shiver, sick with a fever of thought. A gift reserved for the living.

He is of the living dead, never to find peace. The true sinner casts into hell.

Bad Things

People will often ask me, what is it like to go mad. Like I have the answers. I'll tell them, go ask Benjamin. Benjamin is on death row for murdering three innocent people with a kitchen knife on three different occasions in three consecutive days. Like a well-oiled machine.

Benjamin is also my brother. That was five years ago, back when he was fifteen and I eighteen. I was a boy on the verge of adulthood, where life is the quietest before the storm. That was the summer he showed up to family dinner after missing for three days.

Benjamin never talked about what happened.

He even refused to look at the victims' families during his case. My family tried convincing our lawyer that my brother had some type of mental disorder, or that he had been bullied. Anything. However, tragedy takes its toll.

This is five years before I find my first gray hair or watch my grief-stricken mother throw herself out of a window. Five years before I watch my father burst into tears at her funeral.

Benjamin tore our family apart…. For what?

One year ago, I visited my brother for the last time. He sits comfortably in an orange jumpsuit, only nineteen; he looks young for someone scheduled to die.

"Why," I ask him. I must know. Barely able to look at the thing that was my brother. A shiver runs up my spine. In four years, not a single word to anybody. He gives me six.

Then Benjamin shrugs both shoulders, begins to laugh uncontrollably. I watch a guard restrain him, pulling him back through a locked door.

Ten minutes later, outside, a woman mistakes me for an older man. At only twenty-two, I look haggard and sick. I know the horror of life. Benjamin's words run through my head.

"I like to do bad things."

Shut Eye

I took a small hammer, two nails, and a long piece of wood. It was my job to board up the bedroom window and his job to tip the large cabinet in front of the door.

The large cabinet comes crashing down. Woof. Rattling the floorboards. Nobody was getting in or out. Both of us are drenched in sweat. We look at each other, falling back on our haunches on opposite ends of the room. Outside, a warm wind whips through scattered leaves and skinny branches. The werewolf moon is the color of cream, and thick fog is choking the earth with fingers around her throat. He looks at me holding up two fingers, exhausted.

Now there were only two. An hour ago, there were three of us and the day before that, four. One by one until there were just two. I pull the knife out of my left boot and stare at it, admiring the shiny tip of the blade with my index finger. I look over at my friend in the opposite corner. He has his knife out too- with a wise man's grip on the handle.

His eyes are tinged red as are mine. Both of us have our nervous ticks. None of us have slept in five days. The others fell asleep and were murdered. But that is the game. That is why we are also still alive. At first, it was just a stupid game, 'Sleep Deprivation.' Until we decided to place a wager 'Last man standing.' The thing is, none of us figured that the other was hurt for cash as much as the next person, so we decided to bet big.

Both of us had agreed that we would end the game here. We used to play together in this abandoned house as kids looking for ghosts. Soon, one of us would be in for the long sleep. Bobbing back and forth now. I feel like I'm bench-pressing both eyelids. He crawls over with the knife between his teeth. "Shah, go to sleep." He pets the side of my face. "Just a quick… nap, --for a sec--." I ramble. Closing both of my eyes. "Of course, pal," my friend, whispers, bringing the knife up under my chin.

Psycho Killer

"I'd murder somebody, for sure. But what I really want to do most of all is ruin somebodies life. Put a mark on it, you know how dogs piss on trees to claim their territory. I'll do that with this knife, whatcha think?" Philip looks in the downstairs mirror, talking to himself.

The clouds were hidden today, and the sun was out. People were either at the lake or out on a jog with their dog. Philip picked up the knife on the table. It was a day not to be missed.

"I'm going out for a walk, mom, I'll be back in a bit," Philip mutters under his breath, opening the front door. A small woman pokes her head out of the kitchen with a phone next to her ear and a frying pan in the other.

"Well hold on honey, can you pick up a carton of milk from the convenience store; some tomatoes as well. Definitely, don't forget the tomatoes. I'm making your father some lunch. Take the car, okay." She says, throwing him the keys.

Philip quickly puts the knife in his back pocket, scowling.

"Yes mother...," His mother gives him a smile, turning around to continue her phone call.

Philip pulls the car out onto the road, occasionally looking out on the street, people watching.

"Did you know that one in ten people you meet are sociopathic. Absolutely no fucking emotion, what-so-ever." He replies, speaking to nobody, a slight smile forming at the end of his lips.

"Okay-well-maybe that is an exaggeration, but you didn't know that did you. It's easy to assume that something somebody tells you is the truth. That's human nature. But not to me, or a lot of people… and that's the truth."

Philip walks into the convenience store. It's empty, except for a fat man behind the register not paying attention. He gets the milk and a couple of milk duds for himself and places it on the front counter. Philip digs into his pocket for change, remembering all too quickly where he had left the knife.

He looks at the fat man and grins.

"Do you keep a gun behind there?" He murmurs. The fat man barely looks up. "That'll be five dollars, kid." He says, instead focused on the newspaper in his lap. Philip grunts, pulling out the change.

"I bet you don't have one. I bet if some guy tried to rob you, you'd shit your pants, big man." The fat man looks up. "Get the fuck out of here kid." He grunts, shaking his head. The kid waves goodbye, casually walking out the door.

Philip pulls out onto the road again. He repositions the driver's mirror. Looking back at his reflection.

"In case you're dying to know, yes, I planned to kill somebody before. Followed them home. Stood outside their door. I took the leap. But you know why I didn't go through with it? I had a bad feeling about the whole ordeal. Called it off. I'm smart enough not to get caught. I don't let my impulses control me, --

Philip stops at a red light. A man and a woman walk across the crosswalk obviously in a bitter argument. Hand gestures and red faces.

--obviously, some people should try it." He finishes, following them with both eyes.

Philip's phone rings in his pocket, vibrating softly. It was mother. "Hey mom, I just picked up the stuff. I'm headed back now." He talks into the phone.

"Oh, great honey. Well, I am having a couple of people over for drinks. Relators. People interested in the property. Would you mind picking up a couple other things?"

"Mom-come on…" Philip moans, slouching in the seat. "Philip!" She hisses. "Ugh, ok, what do you need mom…" He breathes.

"Well, I need you to stop by the hardware store. Pick up a bottle or two of bleach and some rubber gloves. I'm going to clean up the bathroom." She replies, her tone much lighter than before.

Philip turns the car around, shaking his head. "Love you, mom." He licks both lips, turning off the phone.

An hour later Philip pulls into the driveway, carrying a couple of plastic bags underneath each arm.

He walks into the kitchen and sets the bottles of bleach on the counter and puts the bread and milk in the refrigerator. There are a couple of kitchen knives in the sink and a couple of rags on the floor.

On the kitchen floor are two pairs of sandals, which must have belonged to somebody else. He didn't recognize them. Philip stares at them for a long moment.

"Mother?" he calls out.

Philip hears a couple of footsteps coming down the stairs. His mother walks into the kitchen. She is holding a phone to one ear as usual and is wearing a large cooking apron.

"Thank you, sweetie." She puts the phone down and gives him a kiss on his cheek. Before returning to her conversation.

Philip scratches his head.

The front and back of his mother's apron are covered in red blotches. Bits and pieces of whatever, dried on her apron and had formed into crusty bits that looked like a scab.

His mother turns back around, cradling the phone between her chin and shoulder. She looks over at Philip and quickly takes off the apron, setting it on the counter. Then, she picks up the two big bottles of bleach and walks back upstairs. He hears the bathroom door shut with a bang. Then he hears the bathtub water begin to pour out of the faucet.

Philip picks up the apron and scratches a bit of the red crust of with his finger and smells it.

His mother comes back downstairs, wiping her hands together. She looks at him and smiles, taking the apron from his hands. Back on the phone.

"What is on the apron, mom? Looks like blood." Philip half laughs, scratching the back of his again.

She throws it in the sink. "I was dicing some tomatoes darling, and I accidentally cut myself with the knife. Right here on my damned finger. I bled like a stuck pig." She laughs. Showing him one of her fingers wrapped up in gauze.

Philip takes a step back. "Oh-I just remembered that you wanted me to pick up some tomatoes, I must have forgotten..."

His mother spins her head around, responding quickly. Still on the phone. "Oh-that is right, well I found some." She cheerfully smiles.

"Ok..." Philip bites his lip, pointing towards the shoes on the floor.

Did the people come over?" His mother looks over at the sandals, shaking her head

"People always forget the damnedest things." She bends over and picks them up, seemingly speaking to herself.

Philip watches his mother walk over to the trashcan and toss them in the bin.

"Ok...Mom?" He whispers. Continuing. "Um, I'm just going to go out for a walk now." Philip bites his lip, turning around.

His mother frowns, sighing deeply. "Oh Philip, come here. I won't lie to you anymore. The truth is, the relators were already here when I called you. You weren't supposed to know. I had you run errands, so I knew you would be for sure out for a while. But, I forgot about the sandals, I'm getting old." She laughs, wrapping her arms around him.

Philip awkwardly accepts her hug.

"However sweetheart, I need you to hand me the knife back." She pushes away looking up at him. Arms folded together. "Wha---," Philip murmurs, dazed and confused. "The knife darling, the one in your back pocket." His mother confirms. Philip's face turns red. "Umm." He groans, handing her the knife. She takes it and hugs him again.

"I am sorry Philip. I wasn't chopping tomatoes. Yes, people did come over, but they won't be coming over anymore or going anywhere ever again for that matter. They're dead. One is upstairs dissolving in the bathtub, and the other is in the freezer. But I just want my baby boy to play nice. You promise?" She kisses him on the cheek again.

Philips' mouth hangs open like a gaping hole. The world seems to rest, at this moment. Long and dry. Philips mother looks at him with a quizzical look, seemingly half amused. She puts a hand on her hip.

"Darling, you didn't think you were the only one now did you."

The God Machine

History proves women are more likely to use poison as a weapon of murder.

She prefers to use her hands. She sits back in the driver's seat with her hands on the steering wheel. She is a beautiful woman with thick black hair and black eyes-- underneath a black heart and soul of smoke and fire and brimstone.

While her husband and children sleep alone in their bed's unaware-

Their relationship had become stale like moldy bread. What did he expect from her, a warm dinner and great sex? To cook, clean, and serve while her children cling to both arms? She'd sink slower in quicksand.

She hadn't told her husband about the ninety-six mat-black Impala with tinted windows, metallic bumper, and leather upholstery interior. She also hadn't told him about the murders that followed. She'd paid for the vehicle, and its modifications in cash and kept it in a garage somewhere in the city.

Eventually, the police would catch her, she thought. Or figure that she had taken a second mortgage on their home for her joy ride. Then everything would come to an end; a heap of flaming and twisted metal all the way to hell.

But not tonight.

She puts the car into drive, bright yellow headlights.

The God Machine roars; pulling out of the garage and onto the city street like a dragon emerging from its cave. A monster. She had not envisioned much for herself; the idyllic home, a picket fence.

That was then, this is now. Out here, on the road, midnight hour, she took control of HER life and anyone unlucky enough to cross her path. Tonight, she would play God.

An hour later, The God Machine pulls back into the garage. Its windshield and front bumper of the car is covered in cherry red thick pulp and broken bone. The woman's eyes are wide and delicious. Ecstasy. Outside a bevy of flashing sirens run through stoplights, hurtling themselves towards a familiar crime scene, too late.

The woman works effortlessly, spraying off the front of the Impala with a long snake-like hose where the mess condenses into a cherry milkshake swirl at the end of a bottomless drain. When the car is dried off, she throws a thick tarp on top and turns off the lights.

She takes an Uber home; in an hour her boys will be up for school, and her husband will be in the shower getting ready for work. The woman folds her arms across her lap and smiles, feeling exactly where she needs to be.

The Lost

We were lucky enough before the storm sunk our boat to the bottom of the ocean floor, that we had unhooked the lifeboat. Seven days later we were still lost, the three of us. Of course, there were four people, to begin with. We ate the fourth person. He bled from the ragged holes that used to be his fingers and toes. We were just trying to get a bite to eat. It didn't matter, not to myself, or Fred, nor George.

The body gave us enough food to last another day or two. After we were done, we pushed it over the side to feed the circling fins in the water.

A bloody bubble bath. We watched the whole thing with thick skin, unfazed.

Two days later, Fred closes both of his eyes to take a nap, opposite to me on the raft. George sits back next to him, never taking his eyes off me. How could either of them trust me? I was the one who had persuaded the two to help me get rid of the other guy.

George and Fred Leary were brothers. Dividing them would be almost impossible. Still, I was running out of options. While Fred dozes off, I take a boot off and wiggle my toes. I look over at George, whispering. "I'll offer you one of my toes, for one of your fingers." George licks his lips; he nods, crawling over to me.

Got him. Hook line and sucker.

I grip his arm, lean over—and bite into his wrist, like a chew toy, pulling veins out like frayed electrical wire. He screams. Fred jolts up, just as I throw his brother to the side. "There's nothing you can do for him, Fred." In a moment, George's withering stops, and he goes still in a puddle of blood.

"In the end, we did what we had to do." I lift George's arm, offering his brother first bite. Fred looks at me, then at the corpse and then at the tall sky and lonely seas.

He slowly comes over.

Jim

When Pamela met her first love, she was twenty-one, and he was twenty-five. However, in two years she would have to murder him. He couldn't live past 27.

His name was John Nathaniel. He was a musician. She quickly fell in love with him; he had this way about himself. He wasn't afraid to be different. He reminded her of Jim Morrison, the lead singer for The Doors, and her favorite musician. Jim Morrison also had had a girlfriend named Pamela.

Pamela had found the man she'd been searching for her entire life. Her own Jim. She would be Nathaniel's Pamela. It would be her fairytale ending.

Pamela runs a couple of fingers through his thick black curly hair. "You should grow it out a little, down your shoulders," She teases.

"Like a true rock star?" He proposes, red in the face. He loves her, and he loves how in love with her he is.

"No, like Jim." Pamela hisses. He reaches for a drink, not hearing her. "What was that sweetheart?" Pamela smiles back. "Nothing, baby."

"Love me touch me and tease me," She tells him the first night they make love. "Kiss my ear, and then my neck," she says. She unbuckles the black leather pants she'd bought for him, sliding them around his ankles. Both rock back and forth, together. She places her head on his chest, feeling another man's heart thumping inside, waiting to get out. "Listen to the music," Pamela whispers.

Much later, Pamela surprises him with tickets to Paris for their anniversary.

"A weekend in Paris with my rock star," she kisses him. The two stay in a small apartment and drink wine and make love. She runs him a hot bath. Nathaniel lays down in the bathtub with a wine glass in his left hand. He opens both eyes. Music is playing in the other room. Pamela opens the bathroom door, music floods into the room.

Jim Morrison's voice?

Nathaniel feels tired. He drops the wine glass. Pitching over in the tub, unable to move.

"Help—m," he mumbles, unable to speak. The Rohypnol taking an effect. Pamela leans over and kisses him, pushing his head into the water.

"Jim Morrison died of a fatal drug overdose in his Paris apartment, July 3rd, 1971. Such a tragedy my fantasy."

Pamela chokes back tears, using both of her arms to keep him underneath the water. Her boyfriend stops moving. Pamela lets go, uttering a single shriek.

"I love you, Jim."

Love is a Drug

"Around the time that we both lost our minds is around the time that we got together." I remind her. Don't you remember?

The girl looks back at me with big eyes and a fast beating heart. As I pour another mound of dirt over her body, scooping the shovel into the earth. "Goodbye Nancy, I love you," I whisper. She struggles, kicking her feet. To no avail.

When we were together, Nancy had enjoyed being taken care of; she also had a drug problem. The girl and I lived under the same roof and got high off each other. We were each other's vices.

She didn't work, but I had a job at the post office. Every day after work I would pull up into the driveway and Nancy would be standing in the doorway with a smile attached to her face.

I would get out of the car and kiss her. Put my arms around her waist. We were in love with one another and fed off the drug that was our relationship.

Nancy and I were inseparable. Or so we told one another. Being in love can also be a true lie.

She clung to me like a tick on flesh so that neither of us would end up alone.

However, one day Nancy decided to leave on a gloriously sunny afternoon and didn't look back. There was a handwritten note on the kitchen counter. "I need to love myself again. I think you should try and do the same," It read. She was going to get clean and sober from me.

My first night as a single man, I began my detox. I started to convulse, violently. Imagining myself as a single man and it made me sick. Gripping the bed sheet, clutching my heart. Trying not to think of her.

But I couldn't. I knew if Nancy was out there, I knew I would always be tempted to go back.

I had to find her. We could both find a way to move forward, whatever that was.

When I am finished burying my girlfriend, I toss the shovel aside and sit on top of her tomb. Taking a fresh inhale of air while imagining her gasping her last breath.

Tomorrow, I will get up out of bed and move on with my life. At some point, we must accept change. This is apart of being human.

We must BURY our pasts…and get on with life.

Wolves at the Door

Beautiful black leather gloves, a part of his fantasy for all others involved. A handsome man with an attractive face invites himself over to your house. A charming smile with delicate fingers and wandering big eyes to accompany his voracious appetite for her delicates.

He wants to walk a mile in your shoes and wear your skin like a raincoat. He'll tell you that he understands you and where you come from. We pray to the same god and are afraid of the same monsters, he says. Let me into your home. Every time he plays the game, the stakes are increased.

His eyes thick with lust and a longing for her, he tastes her on his tongue. Regular sex becomes irregular. Often, she would try to fight back, to scratch and claw at his cheek. Natural born sinner. She believes everything that he has told her. Under his weight, she pushes herself into him. He growls like a wolf and devours her whole. In the morning, he picks her out between his teeth.

Leftovers.

Untitled #3

A narrative from your favorite killer, part II

You told me that you loved me when you proposed. Is it a lie?

There is only death. That is a promise that both of us can keep.

But wait, girl. I think that the both of us should not bite down on our relationship cyanide pills just yet.

Let's go for a walk and only stop to pick the flowers and collect sunshine in a glass jar. It will seem like a distant dream when we are far and further into the bush than ever before. But close enough to share the same oxygen.

I will give you a kiss and lay you down on the jungle floor and take off your clothes.

I will hand you a shovel and order you to dig a hole and when you are done to get in the hole, and I will throw the dirt back on top of you.

There will be a search, but you will never be found. People forget quickly. When your friends and family are gone, your name will be forgotten. It will be like you never existed, and everything that you did will be lost forever.

But I will remember. You will be trapped in my head. Your memory will live on through me.

Don't you see that you will never find a better man than me?

I loved you so much that nobody else could have you.

The Finger

Margaret puts her left hand into her jacket pocket, where the human finger is. In front of Margaret is the menu: she had decided on the large chocolate milkshake, onion rings, and Caesar Salad. Her waitress, a plump woman with a soft smile, takes the order to the kitchen. The small diner is empty- except for one couple, an old man and a woman, and a young man who is a student just like herself, hunched over a bowl of warm soup. Witnesses, she reminds herself.

Margaret's waitress brings the chocolate milkshake and food. She takes the finger out of her pocket, looking around. The young man was cute, she thought. He would be the first to help her. Emotional trauma. He would attest to that; hell, he would testify at the trial. A woman once sued McDonald's because the coffee was too hot and won big. This was something else entirely.

Margaret puts the finger into the milkshake and then sits the straw in the milkshake, stirring it like a witches' cauldron. Margaret pretends to pick at the salad; in a minute, when the waitress comes to check on her order, she'll dump the milkshake on the floor and start screaming.

Of course, it wasn't her own finger, such a morbid idea, she thought. That would be crazy, no. It belonged to the dead guy on the motorcycle who had crashed outside her apartment building. There had been a lot of screaming and a lot of blood.

Margaret had been alone. "Help me," the motorist gurgles, gripping the hem of her dress with a bloody hand. A tall piece of glass sticks out of his chest. The wheels of the bike are still spinning. Margaret looks at him. "But, you're already dead," she whispers. The ambulance is loud and on its way.

Margaret sees the finger, lying next to him. She picks it up and looks at it. Her mother had always taught her to recognize an opportunity when it knocks. She puts it in her pocket and walks back inside.

Closer

"I'm almost home, Geraldine thought. Just look up, keep your eyes on the sky and your feet-moving forward". Up ahead the moon continued its lonely dance with strangers, ticking away into the night like a clock. The city is covered in a dark blanket.

Not a blanket for warmth, but something that would be tied around your neck, pulled tightly until your face turned blue and your heart stopped. Geraldine couldn't be sure why she had decided to walk home at this hour.

Now Geraldine could see her house just over the hill. It had to be no more than one hundred steps away. The woman begins to smile, feeling the relief in her shoulders. Everything was going to be all right, she thought. The sun would rise, and tomorrow would be the start of a new day.

"Here we go," Geraldine mutters to herself. One hundred…. ninety-five…ninety, counting her footsteps. She was still scared. The woman looked around, clutching her heart.

Keep going; she reminded herself.

Eighty. Seventy-five. Closer. On the other side of the street was a stranger. Both hands in his pockets, head turned towards Geraldine.

Geraldine pretends not to notice him, instead, picking up her pace. Sixty-five. It's nothing; he's going home just like you. She tells herself. Just another person caught up under the blanket. The stranger is now in tandem with each of her rapid steps. Extending his legs in earnest.

"Go away, please." Geraldine bites her lip. She reaches into her purse for her house key, digging around frantically. Forty-five. The stranger steps off the sidewalk, coming towards her. Geraldine picks both of her feet up and begins to run. Panic was exploding in her chest. Flinging her arms back and forth. Thirty-three. If I turn around, he'll get me, and I know the monster is going to eat me. She thought, her mind working in overdrive.

The woman hears the monster take off after her, growling through its teeth, its hot breath on her neck. "I won't let you," She hollers, dashing across the driveway. Ten steps. Five steps.

She had timed it out perfectly; she was going to make----The woman reaches into her purse pulling out a ring of keys all the same color…Geraldine just stares at her choices. Taking another step to find the right key. One-step too much.

She feels its claw grab her around the neck. Geraldine tries to scream but cannot as the monster moves on top of her, pinning her down.

It begins to feed. Soaking the moon red

The Man in the Nice Clothes

The man in the nice clothes walks up the steps and onto the front porch. He stops in front of the door. Smiling wide.

Life had handed him a lot, but he knew behind every closed-door lies an opportunity. He knocks on the door and takes a step back.

The door opens, another man steps into frame. The man was younger but looked ten years older. His face is scruffy, and his belly is big.

In one hand is a coffee cup and the other is a rolled-up newspaper. "Listen, whatever you are selling, neither of us are interested." The young man begins to shut the door.

"I am not trying to sell you anything. That would mean a price is attached. I just need a minute of your time, which costs absolutely nothing." The salesman replies.

The young man rolls his eyes, closing the door. "Thank you, but I am not interested in what you have to say."

The man in the nice clothes takes a step forward, blocking his foot in front of the door. "I have something I want to give you." He retorts.

"Oh, what is that?" The young man exhales impatiently, tapping his foot.

The man in the nice clothes flashes a million-dollar grin, taking a courtesy bow. Legs crossed, and knees bent. "A pair...of nice clothes." He exclaims proudly.

"I'm afraid you had better try the next house over salesman. I have a couple of suits hanging up in the closet. As soon as you leave, I will put one on and head off to work. Then we will both be wearing nice clothes, won't we." The young man mutters, seemingly irritated.

But the salesman shakes his head.

"No, you don't understand. A very renowned tailor lent me this suit. He told me it was hand stitched with the most delicate thread in the world. So perfectly crafted, I dare say, that it was his entire business. He knew he would never make another like it. So frustrated, he shut down his business and lived on the street in this very suit.

When the tailor lent it to me, it was all he had. The tailor was dying you see. So, in theory, he gave me his life. I must honor and respect that. Now it is my turn. The tailor told me that one day I would have to give my life away, just as he had done, and that that person would give his away, and so on and so forth. So here I am, with a nice pair of clothes for you."

He smiles.

The young man takes a step back, allowing the salesman another inch into his home. His face is pale. "Gh-et out!" He stammers.

However, the salesman puts a thin hand on the young man's shoulder and leans in and gives him a kiss on the cheek. "You're welcome," He whispers. Taking off his hat.

Behind the young man, his wife comes running down the stairs in a bathrobe, toothbrush in hand. "Darling, what is all the fuss?" She moans.

Her husband turns around.

"Call the police!" He yells, pulling on the salesmen. His wife looks at the stranger in her house and runs into the kitchen.

"So now I will hand this suit over, starting with my jacket." The man in the nice clothes removes his jacket and hands it too the young man, who stares in a daze, perplexed.

"What are you doing? Here-take this back now!" The young man retorts. But the man in the nice suit is already beginning to unbutton his shirt. He takes it off and hands the young man, quite literally, the shirt on his back.

"Here my son." He nods, puffing out his naked chest. "This isn't funny! Get off my porch, the police have been called!" The young man banters, shoving the shirtless man out the door.

However, the shirtless man continues to undress, unbuckling his pants. "The tailor who gave me his jacket and shirt also gave me this pair of pants that I am now giving to you." The salesman drops his pants around his ankles. Then he smiles; standing naked on the porch, in glorious flesh for the entire world to see.

The young man stumbles, catching himself. Aghast and pale-faced.

The naked man smiles and opens one of his palms. In the palm is a small razor blade. The orange glint from the morning sun shoots off the metal toothcomb in his palm, twinkling like a fading star in the sky.

The naked man brings the comb up to his throat and presses it against the Adam's apple. Slicing his throat open like a sack of potatoes.

It all happens too fast. There is blood everywhere. Over your shirt, over your shoes, and face. The naked man drops to his knees and then to the floor and onto one side. He dies with both eyes open.

There is about as much screaming, as one would expect. Filling the crisp morning air. The young man stumbles falling on top of the body.

"Help! Help!" He roars, trying to pick himself up. But the screaming does not stop. Half attempts at communication. The salesman looks up at the young man with two smiles. The regular and the one below he had carved for himself.

Tick tock goes the world in slow motion. The color of the grass and the sky begins to mesh together into one. A euphoric sense of the insane.

His wife comes up behind him, adding to the screaming and hollering. She tugs on his arm. A couple of doors down, a neighbor opens the front door, scratching his head.

Now a couple of people are running across the lawn. One of them has his hand on his belt. Another one comes up from behind. Both are dressed in blue. There is a police car in the driveway.

Maybe they are police officers? The young man sees them as slow-moving leopards. Moving spots.

The young man hears a thunk noise. His wife is lying on her back, unconscious. He pushes her off him, peering over the body of the dead man. The dead man's eyeballs roll into the back of their sockets. He reaches out a bloody hand and grasps the young man's leg. A layer of flesh and vocal cord's separate where the dead man drew the knife across his neck to form into a cruel smile. Then the slit begins to speak.

"The tailor had given me all he had. So, in theory, he had given me his life." The body whispers.

Caught in a perpetual insane dream. The young man nods his head, unable to move.

"Now, it is my turn." The dead man whispers.

The world fades.

Side B

12:01 am:

One Minute After Midnight

Dating for the Damned

Dating is just a board game for serial killers. Honestly, look at the fucking thing. In what other professional venue is it socially acceptable to meet strangers? The very idea of dating brings a shiver to my spine, the kind of shiver you get watching a scary movie with the lights off.

Women will admit that meeting someone for the first time can be scary. Women want the man with a well-paying job, good sense of style, movie star grin, and the ability to talk them down from the edge on a rainy afternoon. The perfect man: the funny guy, well-traveled, well-educated, born and raised for one specific purpose in life. For you.

Okay. Now that we have cut through the bullshit with a butter knife let me take the blindfold off your eyelids and remember that everything that you'd been taught is a lie.

The perfect man that you'd imagined is pure fiction. The dirty little secret is that meeting someone new is much like playing a game of Russian roulette with a loaded pistol pressed against your cheek, and my finger is pulling the trigger.

The perfect man is a lie created by attractive men

with ulterior motives. We want to meet you, but we needed a reason to. I'm HIM. I'm the guy that you ladies hear about on TV or in the cheesy romantic comedy. You know the one starring the guy that you wish was your boyfriend. I'll use this to my advantage.

I'll wear a nice tie, comb my hair, and get a socially acceptable job with benefits and assume my new identity.

It's what you were taught as little girls. You are brought up to believe that you deserve a man like me.

For people like me, however; the well-educated, good-looking, socially acceptable bastards who wouldn't mind seeing what your gall-bladder looks like from the inside out are never added into the equation. Is a great looking man ever considered a threat? The media tells you that a person with sharp cheekbone structure and who owns an expensive car couldn't possibly spend their free time butchering women. Preposterous!

Seriously, weren't good-looking individuals meant for so much more than to turn into mass murderers? Or is that what we would want you to believe. If not for my bone structure, who would we know to put on television or incorporate into mass media? To influence the culture of youth, decide when and what to wear or to run our companies. Who would we pin up on our wall, or declare secular division of worship? Who would you have been taught to trust?

The beautiful women that sits across from me smiles at the waiter after he stops to refill our glasses of water. I flash him the "fuck off" smile, and he does just that. You had lost her for only a minute, I remind myself considering her eyes. Now it had come time to play the role that I had been born to play. If only I could remember her name.

We already had quite a night planned. Later we would visit the theater, and even later I would ask her to come home with me so I can show her my surgical kit; which contains my rusty knife used to chisel through flesh and bone. Her name is Janelle, and unbeknownst to her, she is the first "Janelle" that I had ever been with, so I feel like a complete mongrel in slipping up on her name. I'm bored well before our appetizers arrive; twiddling my silver fork on a lone noodle in a bowl of soup imagining it was my rusty knife playing with her spleen.

I'll tell her I am thinking about us and gently massage her palm with my palm. I'm almost too good that I must smile, and she smiles back at me. I am pretty fucking spectacular by the way; in case you were wondering. You must have a clear topic, well-thought-out ideas and still able to listen to her when she believes that she had one. But most importantly what you're saying must grasp her attention.

Just like this. Never apologize for babbling and never shrink mid-story and let your experiences diminish as you search for the right words. Chew the fucking scenery up. Extravagant hand gestures and look at her like you're a fucking marine sniper posted low in the tall, long green grass.

Think of any time you've been to a good film. You must be the main attraction. Discuss your travel and ambition or how you have grown as a person and avoid meaningless conversation such as pop culture references, gossip, or whatever you want to call "water cooler" conversation. Keep the focus on her.

If she is interested in where you're going in your life, she'll most likely go home with you later tonight. Just like the stranger handing out delicious looking pink candy to a child from inside an automobile.

The venue is jammed packed with handsome stranger faces and a full assortment of stories from frolicking lips. All around me I can count them out; at least half a dozen of us seated in the restaurant tonight and a few recognizable faces that run in the same serial killer circle.

You'll have to be sure to take her to the best spot in town. For our dinner tonight, I had begun with the Thai Cucumber Shrimp Appetizer, which composes of sliced cucumbers topped with shrimp and hot chili sauce; easy and fun. Our second course for the evening is the attention grabber.

Lobster tail in a beurre monte, slowly poached in warm butter with plenty of spice for flavor with a side of small new red potatoes drizzled with truffle oil; simple and elegant. Do not forget the Julienne fresh snow peas and carrots cut into julienne matchsticks with a refreshing lemon vinaigrette sauce.

For dessert order the Flourless Chocolate Sponge Cake served in a martini glass topped with whipped cream, chocolate ganache, and toasted nuts. Share the spoon. The women named Janelle excuses herself from the table to use the restroom. I smile, kissing the top of her hand and Janelle or whatever the fuck her name is blushes a drunken raspberry red.

Here's how it goes. Before a meal, you should

order a drink such as a martini or a scotch or bourbon highball. These drinks are cold, light, and get the appetite prepared to receive your meal. Also, provides stellar conversation and game for steering her where you need her to be. Following the meal, you would only want to order a dessert drink, such as brandy, cognac, or some liqueur. These shut down the taste buds to aid in digestion, thus making her feel the need to use the restroom and allow me to make my most crucial move of the night.

She'll excuse herself and hurry off to the ladies' room. Her stiletto heels tapping across the floor like little pins and tiny arms flinging from side to side. Women either will love their heels or hate them. But sometimes; in Janelle's case, they'll try to alter that to fit a guy's height.

As soon as she turns her back, I reach into my coat pocket for the sleeping pill and pop it into her drink on the table. I can tell that Janelle's starting to appreciate the Rohypnol I gave her towards the end of our dinner. She's slurring her words and saying stupid shit, so I figure that it's time to tip the waiter and be on our way.

One can only imagine what's going through her mind right now, well besides the sedative of course. To be honest, I'd admit to not caring. If my plans go well, her opinion won't matter too much come tomorrow morning. I must apologize politely to a couple of the tables as we leave the restaurant hand in hand. Take her home as if you'd ordered her for dinner. Get in the cab with her. Be persistent but not intrusive, women like men who will take charge, they like for you to be the man.

She wraps an arm around my neck and kisses me as our yellow automobile takes off down the street, spewing exhaust fumes and a particular horror story to go. Then we are home. I turn the key in the keyhole, and we are fumbling with each other's clothing as if we were undergraduate students after a night on the town. I tilt her head back to nibble on the ear, both of them. She mumbles something as her tongue rolls out of her mouth like the red carpet at a Hollywood premiere and her eyelids roll up into the back of her head. Janelle falls to her knees.

You'd be surprised how difficult it is to lug a one hundred and fifteen-pound human being by each armpit. I push the door open, dragging her body inside and kick the door closed secluding both off us in my house of horror. Janelle is out cold, so it's easier to snap the handcuffs around her wrists to the bedpost on my bed. Her arms are held high above her head as if she were pleading for mercy and her legs hang off the side of the mattress, so I have to scoop them back on.

While Janelle is passed out, I get up and go behind the kitchen counter to get the rubber gloves beneath the sink and begin to lay out a clear, blue roll of plastic sheet on the tile floor all around the bedroom. She looks so peaceful over there. I take my shoes off and my belt and then my pants, folding them over the back of the futon and finally my shirt before moving into the bathroom to step into the shower.

The warm water hits my face and then my bare skin, washing away all my grime and filth down into the circling drain beneath my feet. It feels good to peel this face off like a Halloween mask that I wear and pretend to fit into this society as if I were playing dress-up like a child.

This is what all of you women want, to be something that you had been told to see. Well, don't complain if you don't like what you see underneath. It might frighten you. I turn off the hot water and step out of the shower stall and into the hallway, drying myself off with a black towel that hangs on the handrail to the stall.

I drop the towel and strut out into the bedroom, newspaper scrunching beneath my bare feet. Janelle's somehow up and about, although her eyelids are heavy and fat. She's pulling on the handcuffs, twisting her body from right till left. There's drool on her chin like a baby before I wipe the spittle away with my left thumb.

Then I'm beside her. Close. The carving knife I'd taken out from the kitchen is hidden behind my back as if it were a bouquet of flowers for a lover waiting to be presented. A sliver of drool drops down onto her neck followed by the heat from the exhaust of my breath. She struggles, half in and out of reality. I reveal the carving knife as if it were the prestige of my magic act.

I can hear her heartbeat through her chest like a ticking bomb about to explode. The carving knife in my left hand shouldn't be there, and I can see her coming to this realization. This does not happen to girls like her, but it did. She's thinking.

"What did I do, I did everything that I had been told to do." The carving knife cuts deep into the inner thigh, spilling bright blood across the sheets and drips down onto the newspaper. I don't even hear her screams, nor do I care.

I'm not the same man that she had agreed to go out with tonight. He's long since dead and she's about to join him.

One Way Ticket

"There's nowhere that you can go, that I wouldn't follow you, I love you." He tells me. "I'd search for you, or tell people that you had gone crazy.

I would get help in my search. "He kisses my forehead.

He was right. There was no place on Earth that he couldn't find me. There was evidence all of my body from previous escapes. Marks, welts, and cigarette burns. He told me later that he had been fair in my punishments.

So, later that night while he slept, I walk into the kitchen and pick up a knife and then slit both of my wrists in the bathtub. I close both of my eyes, feeling at peace. Letting the fog settle in.

He wakes up and runs into the kitchen. As the life pours out of me and into the next, I feel free. In a minute or so, he'll never be able to find me.

He leans down beside me, in my growing pool of blood. Watching me die. My face is cold and pale and so are both of his eyes. He smiles cruelly; petting the side of my face, telling me that he isn't worried. He knows exactly where I'm going to be. All he must do is follow the breadcrumbs.

"Every life comes with a one-way ticket; although some people might get off at the earlier stop, there's only one road into town, sweetheart."

Before I shut both of my eyes for the last time, he presses his tongue into my ear.

He gives me a thought to take with me, I die, terrified.

"I trust, you'll be waiting for me there."

Hunger

She knew that she could not satisfy her hunger. Last month she had brought back ten men, maybe twenty, and eaten them all. From the head to the torso to the tip of the tallest toe and up again.

He sits behind the one-way mirror in her apartment; a fork in his left and a knife in the other. On the table in front of him is a large plate with a large bloody steak. His stomach growls like a tiger in the jungle. Impatience. Is this what he paid for?

Until. She brings back another man for dinner. He watches her kiss this other man; undress him. Whisper in his left ear. Nibble on the ear. Bite it. Rip the left ear off. Scream.

He cuts into the steak. For every bite she takes- removing chunks of bloody flesh from bone- he takes a taste of the bloody steak. After dinner, he pays the bill and drives himself home.

Satisfied.

Daughters

My daughter lives upstairs in a small bedroom with a great view of the morning sunrise. Sometimes, I sleep downstairs, on the couch. I am divorced, seven years, so it is just my daughter and I. I am happy to have her around, to keep me company. We barely ever talk about her future.

My parents live down the street, in a large three-bedroom house. Katherine and Joe are their names. Both are retired and barely speak to me anymore. Not since my sister decided to move away. She left us. It broke my father's heart. As a child, my father would take my sister and me camping. We would set up our campfire, and my father would terrify us with horrific stories. When I grew taller and had children of my own, I decided to continue the tradition.

I roll over onto my stomach, fumbling around for the flashlight. I put on my boots and unzip my tent flap, stepping outside. The midnight wind licks my ears, and the moon is round. The boots that I am wearing are my fathers, given to me on my thirteenth birthday. "One day, you'll be in my shoes, and you'll have a family to raise," He would lay a hand on my shoulder. "If you have a daughter, remember that you are the first man in her life. Show her how to love," Father smiles.

My daughter is asleep in the other tent, on her side. I lay down next to her, breathing through my nose.

She stirs in her sleep. I close both eyes. Forty years ago, I opened both eyes, peeping my head out of my tent.

The tent next to mine rocks back and forth. From the outside, I see what looks like the shadowy figure of a hideous spider with many legs, crawling across the ceiling. My heart is pounding. The spider beast sounds like my sister. Screaming. A part of the tent flap is down, giving me a peek into the monster's cave. My father is on top of my sister. A mesh of pale flesh and fast breathing. He talks to me later. Remembering his words, I give him a hug.

But now I must take off my pants. It is my turn to give love back.

My own daughter turns around, facing me. The night is silent. "I love you, you know that," I whisper, slipping a hand on top off her breast. She nods. "Yes father," She says, a tear rolling down her cheek.

Under the Silver Lake

A narrative from your favorite killer, part I

She could feel her murderer tighten his hands around her throat. Squeezing the last bit of life from her body. The woman begins to kick her legs.

"I'm going to die. I'm going to die, n--," Her mind races back and forth.

"Stop trying to reach for the moon, honey. Sink. Sink. Down towards the ocean floor." He whispers in her ear.

The woman's eyes roll up into the back of her head. Gone.

"Can your toes touch the bottom yet?" He replies, patting the back of her head.

Mother

All Leonardo Cuffin can think about is a warm cup of coffee. A couple of people in the coffee shop look down at their laptops or pretend to bite their tongue when he walks in. A couple of children tug on their parent's sleeves. Leonardo grins, adjusting the platinum blonde wig on top of his head and smoothes out his dress with both hands, he blows the kids a kiss.

The kids turn red and turn around. He knows that nobody understands, but he does not care. Leonardo was named after Leonardo da Vinci, the famous entrepreneur, and artist. His mother told him on his tenth birthday, that he was a painter with a blank canvas, and that his choices would be the brush strokes. She did the best with a young Leonardo.

A year later, Angela Cuffin was diagnosed with leukemia. Leonardo's mother was cremated, and her ashes were kept in a small platinum urn over the fireplace. Leonardo took a small scoop of his mother from the urn and put her in a little tin lunchbox when nobody was looking.

He put the lunchbox in a sock drawer in his room. He wanted her close. Over the next couple of weeks, Leonardo heard his mother's voice, coming from the sock drawer. She told him what a good boy he had been, "I need you," Angela says. So, young Leonardo dumps her ashes onto his desk. He goes downstairs; to the kitchen and comes back with a straw and snorts the rest of his mother's ashes.

When he is done, he looks up into his bedroom mirror, at his reflection. He smiles cruelly, blowing himself a kiss. "Hello sweetheart," she says.

Leonardo walks up to the counter in the coffee shop and orders a hot coffee. She taps her painted fingernails on top of the counter. The cashier does not look at her, mumbling. "What is the name of the order?" Leonardo smiles, "Angela," She says.

Do You Miss Her Yet

"My wife died about ten years ago, and I want to see her again," a voice whispers through the phone.

If you were to picture a face to go with the voice, you might draw an old man with tiny beady eyes and dark blue veiny hands.

The young man puts down the phone, looking around the room. The room is quiet, and the windows are shut. A secret couldn't get out if it tried.

"Who is this?" The young man mutters, nervously tapping his foot.

"The man who misses his dead wife weren't you listening." Croaks the voice on the other end of the phone.

"Listen whoever you are, we don't appreciate prank callers." The young man shakes his head.

"Don't hang up on me or you'll miss her too—," the voice gargles. Click. The young man hangs up the phone.

His girlfriend comes up behind him and wraps her arms around his waist. "Who was it, sweetie?" She replies, giving the young man a kiss on the cheek.

"Just a prank I suppose." He nods. "That's odd, have we ever had one before?" She replies. "No." The young man scratches his head. Half laughing.

"Well dinner is ready sweetheart, come on downstairs." She gives him another peck on the cheek. Then backs out of the room.

"Ok-babe…" The young man exhales, looking at the phone in his hand for a long second.

He hears a loud thud behind him, like a sack of bricks hitting the ground.

His girlfriend is laying on the floor, one arm over the other. There is dark blood coming from her lips, ears, eyes, and mouth. Pouring out like a stuck pig.

The young man begins to scream hysterically, dropping the phone. "Oh my god, oh my god!" He falls to his knees, cradling her head between his knees.

"Somebody help! Help!" He screams, his echoes bouncing off the walls. The young man picks up the phone, stumbling to his feet.

His fingers dialing in for help. 9 one on—

The phone rings, buzzing in his hand. He looks down at the screen. Unknown number.

For some reason unbeknownst to the universe, he answers it. Putting the phone to his ear.

"Your girlfriend died about ten seconds ago, do you miss her yet." The voice replies.

The Stories

I grew up in a small home with just my father and me.

Right before bedtime, my father and I would sit next to a warm fire, and he would read a bedtime story to me. He always told the same stories. He would tell me horrific bloody tales about a monster that lives under the floorboards.

"It had been here long before you and me. If you believe that this house is ours, you are mistaken. We are simply paying rent to a creature far more treacherous than anything you could ever imagine," He would say.

The way my father would describe it left me with goosebumps all over my arms and a headful of bad dreams.

"Our monster has breath that reeks and a hungry appetite for women. What do you think happened to your mother?" My father would remind me.

My heart would pound in my chest. "She tried her hardest to fight the monster, but in the end, it wasn't enough…" I whisper.

My father would begin to cry. Tears falling down both cheeks, like cascading rain on a tin rooftop. "She left the both of us. I know you wouldn't".

After supper, my father is in the kitchen finishing up the last of the beer in the case. His eyes are droopy, and his body is no longer his own. He pivots from side to side like the walking dead.

While I am upstairs underneath my cover, with a flashlight in one hand. I cannot sleep.

Sometime later. After the midnight moon has taken over and the echoes of the former day are but a forgotten memory. When our house is a house of the dead.

I can hear it, coming up the stairs. Creak. I turn off the flashlight; both of my hands are shaking. Creak.

There it is, there is a shadow underneath the door. I roll underneath the cover, scooping my legs into a fetal position. The door handle turns, slowly.

My father hobbles into the room. One hand down the front of his pants-leg. Rubbing himself. He is clinging with sweat; his face is the color of dirty wedding cake. His breath reeks of alcohol.

The monster pins me onto my back, with bits of saliva and nostril exhaust hitting my neck. Its odor reeks of liquor and beer and its eyes are as black as tar. Its tail flickers between its hindquarters. I try to utter a scream, but my father cannot hear me.

The liquid monster has swallowed my father whole. The monster decides to use my father's hands to rip at my clothes, holding me to the bed. The night goes black.

A Horror Story

Mr. Midnight, who is old and ugly, lived alone in a house at the end of the block. He did until he admitted to murdering a boy. I was thirteen and the other boy, my friend, was twelve, old enough to know not to take candy from strangers. Nobody ever said anything about your neighbor.

I imagine he was counting on that trust. After murdering my friend in front of me, Mr. Midnight confesses, like an open book; a horror story. He tells me about the other missing children and that he always murders one child in front of the other. One dies, and the other child helps bury him. Somehow, I manage to escape, with Mr. Midnight waving a knife at my back.

Horrified, I go to the police to tell my story. "We have never heard of a Mr. Midnight, the police say. Nobody has lived in that house for years". A young officer with a boy my age raises his hand;

"I'll consider it." He believes me.

I imagine now, looking back, I was counting on that trust. The officer searches the house and finds the sleeping bag I left there, and a couple of tin pots on a hot stove that I left on, the house is filthy; scurrying rats, and leaky pipes. The police can't believe it; I am asked to give a sketch artist a description of Mr. Midnight. A day later, a hiker finds a body in the woods. My friend.

However, sets of fingerprints found around the throat of the body. Mine.

The police question me; Inside I'm smiling, outside, different, I'm acting. I add detail to my story. "Truth is, he likes to watch one boy murder the other, and then that child helps BURY the other" I choke up tears. Everyone falls for it. Pale face and teary-eyed. The hunt is on. Our town is on the national news, look out for a madman!

He'll get you, my children. Is he under your bed, or is Mr. Midnight hiding in the closet? Shovel and knife in hand. The legend continues to grow and grow.

Everybody remembers the murder victim, but nobody remembers his friend. Maybe I was counting on that.

Years later, my friends' murderer, Mr. Midnight, is still at large. I doubt they'll ever find him. But that's all anybody ever wants to hear, isn't it, a good story.

A Love Story

The mountaintop overlooks the stormy seas; crashing and bellowing waves echo the tortured soul. Two lovers quarrel over life. A love story as old as time itself. Her lips are blue and her tongue firecracker red.

When I pulled the young woman from the water, she hisses and spits at me like a serpent. Death was what she was looking for, but I wouldn't let her go.

I couldn't let the woman I loved try and end her life like this. There might have been a chance she would be picked up by a boat or a passing fishing trawler. She would live another day but forever be changed. I had to get to her before anybody else did.

The cold ocean tide longs to pull us both in with its icy grip, tugging at our ankles like an irritated newborn.

The woman reaches out her hand towards the horizon begging me to cast her away. I carry her back to my car and lay her down in the passenger seat, petting her head. She looks out the window in a daze.

Then I start the car and begin the climb all the way back up the mountaintop. The road turns and twists but I hug the silver guardrail with my foot on the accelerator.

When we reach the top off the cliff, it begins to rain small teardrops down from the sky. I turn off the engine and open the passenger door. Then I take her hand and guide her to the edge of the cliff.

A once scenic view for lovers.

I urge her the will to live on. If only for the moment. "Look at me," I whispered, cupping my hands underneath her chin. "Darling, out there." I then point a crooked finger, showing a passing boat in the distance.

"Don't you see you wouldn't have succeeded. There are always boats patrolling back and forth. No matter how hard you tried it was not the right time for you to die." I reply, holding my woman tight.

But she struggles, the tears running down her cheek. I put a hand on her neck. On the back of her neck is a collision of black and blue bruises. Evidence of our relationship.

The same hand had now clenched itself into a tight fist. Something we were both used too. But I relax the fist.

"You don't control me anymore. My life is not anybody's to decide." She shudders, pulling away. But I continue to hold on. I run my hand around her collarbone, peeling back her shirt. It is worse than I remember. Too bad I enjoyed most of it.

"Why don't you just let me go!"? She screams, kicking and scratching at my chest. The boat is now passing around the lighthouse and out of sight. The air is still, and not a single bird is chirping.

"Okay," I reply, give her a kiss on the forehead, and then push her off the cliff. She screams all the way down. Then I breathe in through my nostrils and take a step forward peering over the edge.

Her body is on the bloody rocks below. The body

stares back up at me through a pair of empty eyes and inexistent conscience.

I watch for a moment as the mighty waves pick up the scent and hurl itself into the rocks, knocking her about. Then catapults the body from the rocks and into the deep blue sea.

I turn my eyes from side to side. No more patrolling boats or fisherman to come to the rescue. That is what I had been counting on.

I can't help but smile. "No matter how hard you tried, it was not the right time to die-

Watching a final gargantuan wave take the body under, where it would never be found.

Whatever mark or burn or else I had done to her that was evidence of our relationship had been washed away.

- But now it is." I retort, climbing back into the car.

The Bombs

Jon Forrester never left his room. Which was common for a writer. The only times were for a smoke, or too lie up on the roof and watch the planes fly by.

The planes were headed somewhere important. Off to burn a couple of traitors, no doubt.

Anybody with two functioning eyeballs could see the bombs hanging off the belly of the machines. End of the world shit.

Anybody with a brain knew that the taste of sulfur and gas in the air wasn't natural. Nor was the way the skyline would light up like an orange balloon, and then change back to blue, as quickly as it had come.

Jon goes back inside to complete the story after he has finished the cigarette. Another plane flies by, buzzing the tall pine trees. Shaking the house. The metal tin pots and pans that hang on the wall inside the kitchen shake back and forth.

Jon sits down at his desk, biting the eraser part of the pencil with his teeth. Time seems to tick by like the gentle touch of a lover, slowly and delicately. On the wall is a calendar, with a date circled. That was when the book was due.

This time, the whole world shakes. Including his chair, the desk, and the floorboards. Bits of sawdust fall onto his shoulders. "Fuck me," He yells, standing up. Raises a fist in the air.

Across the street, the neighbor's dog begins to bark, loud, like a tornado siren. Jumping up and down on its hindquarters. Obviously challenging the incoming fighter jet.

Jon opens the window, and begins to bark, just like the dog. Snarling and shaking his head. The dog turns around, wagging its tail. "You don't even realize who you're barking at, you stupid mutt," Jon yells, ducking his head back inside. He takes a deep breath, blowing hot exhaust out each nostril.

Jon closes both of his eyes. Holding the pencil over the paper. Think dammit. Think. The house rattles, again. On fucking cue, the dog begins to celebrate, even louder. Jon breaks the pencil in half, storming out of the room, and out the front door of the house.

The dog pulls on its leash, which is around a silver pole stuck into the ground. "Fuck you!" Jon leans over, yelling at the dog's face. The dog runs away, towards another part of its yard, continuing its bark.

"It's gone, you mu--," Jon looks up, into the sky. His mouth drops. His heart begins to beat faster and faster. The plane that had just passed by turns around and starts to fly back this way. Circling in the air. Life moves in slow motion.

Jon backs up, step by step. Waving both of his hands at the dog. "Shut up, shut up!" He screams. Starting to run backward. Right as the plane passes overhead, something falls out beneath its steel belly. Dropping fast, towards the earth.

Jon sprints across the street, pumping both of his arms like a windmill. The muscles in his neck straining.

His background noise is a mixture of barking, and the wind shooting past his ears.

The bomb falls through toward the earth, landing right on top of the dog. Driving the mutt's carcass ten foot into the dirt. A messy mixture of strewn up bits and fur. Then, the bomb goes off.

Further down the road, Jon is knocked off his feet, skidding alongside the pavement. The blast is deafening, like standing next to the speakers at a rock show, and the air is immediately a microwave. He loses consciousness.

Jon slowly opens both eyes, pushing off a couple of wooden boards and other miscellaneous items off his back. What looked like to be bits of a house. Both of his arms, legs, and face is covered in black soot. A couple of people are on the road, wobbling around, dazed and confused.

Jon dusts himself off, sighing heavily. Not saying a word. The blast had been big enough to leave a wide steaming crater that used to be the neighbor's home. Sizzling like a well-cooked steak. He turns around, walking through the rubble that used to be his home.

He finds his chair, digging through a pile of rubble. Sitting back. The world is at an empty peace. Jon lifts his head, watching a bonfire of smoke regurgitate itself into the stratosphere. Quiet. Finally.

A tiny grin begins to forms at the corner of his mouth. Time to look for that damn pencil.

The Following

A narrative from your favorite killer, part III

It's not what you think; we are not all murderers. Sometimes we follow you home. Not on purpose, just coincidence. If somebody gets out of their car when you get out of yours, perhaps they live across the street.

Do not be alarmed.

If you notice somebody following you up to your door, perhaps they used to live here; and are reminiscing in their head. Treat them as citizens, not as a trespasser.

If somebody initiates conversation on your doorstep, smile back and be friendly. Perhaps, once you look at them up close, you will recognize a childhood friend. A familiar face.

If not, you are probably wrong. Life is about choices.

Choose to make the right one.

Nobody would ask to come inside if they didn't know who you were, would they? Think about it. So, you let the right one in.

"Well done." He smiles, cruelly. Do not be alarmed; he is probably just happy to see you. Now he pulls out a sharp knife from his pocket and tells you that he has murdered before.

I know what you're thinking. Relax; they were probably bad people anyways.

Then he informs you that you are his next victim. Hmm. Let me think about this one for a second. So, you turn around and try to run. He catches you and brings the knife up towards your throat.

Damn, well you got me here.

But believe me. Sometimes you are followed home. Not on purpose, just coincidence. It's not what you think; we are not all murderers.

But this one sure fucking is.

Twenty Years On

My husband told me that he had packed his bags and that he would be leaving in the morning. He assured me he would be taking the rest of his knives, the shovels, and the two bodies he keeps in the basement freezer.

He tells me he no longer feels utterly comfortable as my husband or being the father of our children. He no longer thinks about our family as much as killing.

I'm living with a real-life monster. This wasn't the man I had married twenty years ago either if you were dissecting my particular taste of men. When some men turn forty, there is a new automobile in the driveway or frequent trips to the gymnasium or that flirty encounter with the secretary at work. My husband found another mid-life vice.

Looking back now, I would have been fine with the car or the secretary. Believe me. It would be a godsend compared to this hellish nightmare. Compared to living with a lunatic. He tells me that he wants to make a name for himself just like his idols Gacy, Bundy, and Lector.

I've cried a lot lately, thinking of a man I once loved. He's gone now. Down the road in the driver's seat of a parked blue Pinto headed west with a sick dream. When I told him, I would give him a twenty-four-hour head start before I call the police, he smiled and told me he loved me. He hadn't told me that in years.

I'm just cooperating. As soon as he's out of sight, I pull out my phone.

Masks

Tiny bits of early morning orange sunshine slice through the boy's window curtain like an open sore. He opens both of his eyes, coming into reality. Leaving the dream world for an even more fantastical land.

Around the corner at the end of the block, the yellow school bus is making its early morning pit stops. Children are getting up and ready for the day.

The wood alarm clock goes off, wiggling back and forth on the dresser. The boy reaches his hand out and slaps it off. Jeremy wipes the sleep from his eyes, as the world comes to focus. Still half blurry like an old VHS tape.

He kicks himself out of bed, planting his feet on the cold floor. He puts on a shirt and a pair of jeans and musters up a half smile.

Ten minutes later, Jeremy walks out of the bathroom with a toothbrush in his mouth, and a backpack slung over his shoulder. He carries himself down the stairs and into the kitchen for breakfast with the bravado you would expect from a twelve-year-old this early in the morning.

One hand scratching his stomach.

Jeremy can smell the breakfast on the stove and hear the pop and hiss of the bacon in the pan. The boys' family is in the kitchen.

His mother is standing in front of the stove, with her back to him, finishing the breakfast. Whistling a familiar tune. While his sister and father are seated at the table.

Jeremy's older sister sits with both of her hands clasped together and her head facing down towards her plate. This morning her hair is done up.

He stops and stares at his younger sister. Why the weird face, he wonders?

Jeremy's father is hidden behind a newspaper, held apart by two chubby hands. There is a small steaming cup of coffee in front of him. Both of his legs are crossed underneath the table.

"Morning," Jeremy says groggily, pulling out a chair for himself. His father unfolds the newspaper.

"Good morning son," He replies. Picking up the cup of coffee and bringing it to his lips.

Jeremy looks up at his father. His lower lip falls to the floor. The person at the table is not his father. But he wears his father's clothes and is holding his father's mug. He is also wearing his father's face. The person is wearing a rubber mask with two rubber eyes, a mouth-hole, a nose, and two ears that look exactly like his father's features. It seemed like the type of rubber mask that Jeremy would wear for Halloween.

Jeremy bites his lip. His heartbeat exhilarates in his chest. He looks over at his sister. She looks up at him. Her face is a pale white color, and her eyes are two beady black balls of adrenaline. His sister mouths something with her lips. "Help…"

"Um…" Jeremy breathes, scratching his head. "What's the matter son," The person in the father mask inquires, sitting back in the seat.

He is a big man with a bigger gut that hangs down below his waist. Unlike the rubber mask, the man's voice sounds nothing like his fathers. His voice is raspy and deep, like a broken record player.

Jeremy just sits still, unable to move. Their mother turns around, balancing a couple of plates in between her arms. She pivots around the table, placing a plate in front of Jeremy.

The boy takes a long hard look at the runny eggs and bacon on his plate, and then up at the woman wearing his mother's face.

The woman is also wearing a rubber mask, but this one looks like his mother's face, with her delicate features. A tuff of brown hair sticks out the top of the mask, like a mole sticking its head from the dirt.

Jeremy bites his lip, looking around the room. "Mom, Dad." He calls out.

The two figures sitting at the table looks at one another, scratching their heads. "Yes, Jeremy." The two figures retort.

Jeremy gives a half-laugh, giving his sister a look. "What's going on, is this some joke?" He whispers. She does not respond. Instead, she continues to stare at her plate. "Jus-be-quiet, they'll hurt us--," His sister mumbles.

Jeremy stands up, taking a couple of steps backward. "Ok, Mom…Dad, where are you!" He screams.

"Jeremy! Stop this, you're acting ridiculous."
The figure in the father mask hisses, slapping the table.

"What did you do with them!" Jeremy says, his
heart beating in his chest.

The woman wearing his mother's face screams
back. Covering her face with her hands. "Why couldn't
you just be a good boy!"?

Father mask steps around the table, heading
towards Jeremy. "Come here, you're upsetting your
mother."

But Jeremy grabs his sister by the arm, pulling
her out of the chair. "Run!" He yells.

The two scrambles through the kitchen and into
the living room, towards the front door. His sister wraps
her hands around the doorknob trying to turn it.

"It's bolted shut," She screams, hysterically.
They can both hear the woman in the kitchen still crying,
sobbing uncontrollably.

Jeremy takes a looks around. Eyes wide open.

The figure wearing his father's face peers around
the corner, grabbing his sister by one of her pigtails. She
screams as he drags her away.

"Jeremy!" She hollers, kicking her legs and
torso. The figure huffs and puffs, flinging her back and
forth like a rag doll. "One-big-happy family," He grins,
pulling her into the kitchen

Gone.

Jeremy goes for a window. The boy tries to lift
the window up but cannot. "Urh- "He grits. Taking a
closer look. A couple of nails had been crudely

hammered in on the bottom of the window latch. Sticking out like a broken bone.

He turns his head around, barely able to control his breath. Taking off again, this time back up the staircase, up towards his room. Jeremy had never moved so quick, hopping over the couch and up the steps. His feet pounding the floor.

The big man appears from out of the kitchen doorway again. Popping up like an animatronic on a scary theme park ride.

Jeremy feels something grab his foot. He looks down. "Come here-boy!" The fat man shouts, but Jeremy pushes him off, continuing up the steps.

He makes it too his room, slamming the door shut. The boy turns the lock on the door. Then scurries up to his bedroom window, standing on the bed. There were no nails under the window latch.

Jeremy shuts both eyes, praying for something that wouldn't happen.

"Please, please…" He whispers. He gets the window about half a foot up.

The boy screams through the crack in the window. Fresh outside air hitting his cheeks. Jeremy sees the bright yellow school bus turn the corner, coming onto his street. "Help, Help!" He moans.

There is a loud thud against the bedroom door. Another. "I'm coming in boy, and you are in big trouble!" The top half of the door breaks off its hinges.

Jeremy jumps off the bed just as father mask wraps its arms around his body, throwing him to the ground.

The big man pushes his weight on top of the boy, pushing him back onto the bed. Breathing hard through both nostrils.

"Lie still and keep your mouth shut." He grits, pushing his tongue into the boy's ear. Jeremy shuts both of his eyes, trying not to blackout. He nods his head.

"Good, now we are both going to get up, and you're going to follow me downstairs. No kicking, running away, or any nonsense. Otherwise, we'll have your sister for dinner…

I bet- (He inhales) … she tastes delicious." The big man replies, gasping between each sentence.

Jeremy nods his head again, tears slipping out of each eye and onto his cheek. The big man rolls off the boy, stumbling to his feet. As he takes a deep breath after breath, his belly wobbles up and down.

Jeremy stands up with his head tilted towards the floor. The two of them walk out of the room and down the stairs, while the big man's hand rests firmly on his shoulder.

When the two of them get to the kitchen, it is empty. The big man pulls out a chair. "Sit." He orders Jeremy, pointing a chubby finger. The boy takes a seat.

"Where is my sister," Jeremy whispers, lifting his head up. Father mask shakes his head, signaling for the boy to be quiet.

In the back of the house, a door slams shut. Then a pitter-patter of feet is heard moving through the hallway. The woman in the rubber mask appears in the kitchen, wiping her hands on the kitchen apron tied around her waist.

"You've been a naughty boy this morning. Haven't you." She wiggles at finger at Jeremy.

"Where is my sister!" Jeremy replies, biting his lip. The woman looks at Jeremy and then at her partner, whispering in his ear. He nods his head before the two of them turn and look at the boy, both smiling.

"Your sister is feeling a bit reluctant to be a part of our family. Just give her some time; I'm sure that she will come around. "The woman retorts, taking a seat. She reaches out and grasps Jeremy's hand, smoothing it over as if it were the house cat. But Jeremy shakes her hand away, standing up.

"What did you do to her!" He screams.

Jeremy picks up the chair he was sitting on, positioning it as a shield and potential weapon.

The man takes a step back, curling one hand into a mean fist. "What do you think you're going to do with that, boy?" The woman sits back in the chair, folding her arms together.

"Tell me where she is…that she is okay." Jeremy stutters, jabbing the chair in their direction. The woman gets up, straightening her back. She turns around, whispering in her partner's ear again.

He nods his head, releasing the balled fist. The woman walks past him and into the living room. She takes a seat on the family sofa and turns on the television, beginning to flick through different channels.

While the man walks up to Jeremy and snatches the chair out of his grip as effortlessly as the boy had picked it up. He puts the chair down and grabs Jeremy by the wrist, forcing him down out of the kitchen and down the hallway.

"No!" Jeremy shouts, trying to pull away. "I told you kid, but you wouldn't listen." The man renounces, pulling the boy in close.

He takes Jeremy through the house and out into the backyard. Which is a wistful arena of green leaf and twisted dirt and route. The big man tosses the boy onto the grass, dusting his hands together.

The big man points a chubby finger around a corner of the home. Follow me, it says. But be quiet.

The two take a walk around the home, stopping in front of a grey door carved into the ground. The cellar door is bolted shut with a long thin chain. Jeremy had been down the storm cellar a couple of times in his life. He closes both of his eyes, trying to forget.

His father would wake him up in the middle of the night, and his sister and mother would be in the hallway with raincoats over their shoulders. Outside, the wicked roll call of the storm sirens would be going off, heeding whoever wishes not to be blown away by a tornado retreat into their storm cellar. Which was one of the mere conveniences of living in mid-western America.

Every house in the neighborhood had one.

When Jeremy and his family had to retreat down the rabbit hole, each family member was responsible for an emergency item. If his sister had to get the batteries for the flashlight, then he would bring down the radio or the plastic chairs for the family to sit in.

His father would undo the thin chain and heave open the cellar door, lifting it up onto one side. He would have a flashlight in one hand, and another hand on his wife's back while the wind and rain paltered their faces.

"Downstairs Jeremy," He would yell, handing his son the flashlight. Jeremy would turn the flashlight on and point it into the cellar. It was always dark, and the room smelled of soot and dust.

A rat or two usually scurries across his feet, waggling their tails. Jeremy would take a long hard look into the cellar and feel the beating of his heart in his chest. "I don't want to father!" He would scream, shaking his head. The air is thick with moisture and dread.

"Jeremy! Help your mother and sister! Get down there and set up the chairs." His father replies, urging his son. Instead, Jeremy's hand shudders with the flashlight as he descends each step further down the rabbit hole. His lungs gasping for breath, he shuts both eyes. Lunging forward, one footstep at a time.

When he feels the solid ground under his boots, Jeremy shines the flashlight around with a shaky hand. Another rat scurries across his feet. He jumps away, backing up against a far corner of the cellar.

"Breathe, just breathe." He reminds himself, re-opening both eyes. His mother and sister are already down here with him, both huddled together. Jeremy's father is the last one down, swinging the cellar door over his head.

Clang.

Jeremy drops the flashlight. He now stands in complete darkness, fumbling around for the flashlight.

"Jeremy! I can't see." His father would scream, banging on the door.

"I'm sorry, I got-it," Jeremy replies, dropping to both knees. It takes him a couple seconds to find the flashlight, scooping it up with both hands.

Click. He turns the light back on.

A large rat now sits on the end of the flashlight. With black whirlpool eyes and a fidgety snout. The rat looks up at the boy, and then jumps from the handle of the flashlight onto the boy's arm, before digging its claws into the flesh of his arm.

Jeremy screams, tossing his head back. As the monster of fear envelops him, taking over from whatever sanity left inside the pit of his lungs. The world goes black.

Jeremy opens both of his eyes again, steadying himself. The big man leans over and unlocks the cellar door, gripping a couple of fat sausage fingers around the door handle.

"Wait! Don't open it." Jeremy retorts, taking a step back.

The big man looks over at him and grins, his expression tightening the rubber mask around his face. He lifts the door swinging it over onto one side. There is a gust of dust and air that hits his face.

The big man grabs the boy by the arm, while the boy kicks his feet out, wailing back and forth.

"Jeremy, help your mother and sister out. Get down there and set up the chairs!" The big man bellows, half laughing. Using his father's voice.

Then, the big man drops him in front of the door, pressing his foot into the boy's back effectively pinning him to the grass. He brings out a flashlight and shines it down the cellar, waving it back and forth.

Jeremy lifts his head, eyes wide. He begins to scream.

At the bottom of the cellar are a couple of people tied to some chairs. There is rope around their ankles and torso and silver duct tape around their mouths. Jeremy's father, mother, and sister struggle in their binds moving back and forth. Their clothes had been removed, except for their underwear and a pair of socks on their feet.

His family looks up at Jeremy pleading through their restraints.

A rat scurries across the floor and onto his sister's lap. She screams helplessly.

The big man laughs, reaching over and slamming the cellar door shut. He lets his foot off Jeremy's back; watching the child slowly roll over, tears cascading down his face.

"Don't make me go down there-I don't want to..." Jeremy snorts, tears and snot mixing together into a magic potion. The big man leans over, blowing smoke into Jeremy's face. "I did exactly as you asked, boy. You see that your family is together. But you seem a lot happier up here, aren't you?"

Jeremy picks himself up and then wipes his nose. He nods his head, never once looking back at the cellar.

"Good." The big man smiles, giving Jeremy a kiss on the forehead. He puts a hand on the boy's shoulder, leading him back inside.

Jeremy shuffles into the living room, head held low, with both arms swinging by his side.

The woman wearing his mother's face gets up off the couch and comes over, wrapping her arms around him. "Oh, my boy, you are so precious." She exclaims, gently rocking him back and forth. The big man takes a seat on the other end of the couch, picking up the remote from in between the seat cushion. He presses a button on the remote and begins to flip from station to station.

Jeremy sits down on the couch in between the woman and the big man, hands clasped over both knees. The big man reaches an arm across the couch, scooping his wife and son together into one tight ball.

One happy family.

Serial Killer Land

Twisting the cruel, cold knife into his side is blissful. He's a beggar on the sidewalk. He won't be missed by a world that cast him aside. I'm barely alive at this point, choking on my own fumes. Adrenaline rushes through my veins lifting me higher than ever. When he falls to the dirt, he'll be dead then, and I'll be known as a murderer.

It's a small price to pay for enlightenment. There is a moment after death when the spirit leaves the body. Both of my eyes go up, up further into the endless blue sky imagining the beggar smiling back down at me, thanking me. There is a roof over his head and shoes on his feet.

"In my Father's house are many rooms. If it were not so, would I have told you that I go to prepare a place for you?" John 14:2

I close the book in my hands. This morning, God told me to pack my bags. I had been chosen for a mission that nobody would understand. Having never traveled anywhere let alone outside of my city I'm grateful.

A plane ticket to Serial Killer Land cost about as much as you need to be there.

The Costume

October thirty-first is the only day of the year where you can be anyone you want to be. Our society obsesses over the obscene and the cruel. We watch hit television shows about serial killers and other monsters. Halloween is the day we can dress up in their skin. Where everybody is someone else. Where children ignore parental advice and collect bucket full's of candy from older men and women that they barely know.

I am a father of two young children with a beautiful wife. By all means, I am the standard red-blooded American male. I pretend to enjoy monogamy and my job. I'm normal. On the outside.

Too bad, every day of my life I struggle with an oblique dark fantasy that only people one day a year pretend to be. I am nothing like the man that you know. Pain is my gift. Without it, my victims would not know fear or pity. Without fear, there would be no humility. Then, every man and women would become me. A monster. The tie and briefcase are my Halloween costume. Inside, I live October thirty first every single day of my life.

This year, I have decided to embrace October thirty first. Every year, the company that I work for hosts a costume party. There will be a lot of drinking and gossip. There will be talk of the man, standing in the corner, all to himself. Wearing the same company tie, slacks, and carrying the leather attaché case that he takes to work and to the party.

At the end of the night, there is a costume contest. I'll smile and applaud the winner. Of course, nobody will understand. If they really knew, I would win the contest unanimously. I imagine, more so out of fear.

Dreams Do Come True

Sometimes a recurring dream will feel as real as the air you breathe. It will wrap its hands around your throat and continue to squeeze.

This particular nightmare begins when I am a boy. When I am the same age as my own children. I feel the tip of the old man's fingers run through my hair. His breath is cold on my cheek where it should be warm. His grin is a cavern of dirty steak knives that could devour my flesh and slurp the skin right off my bone.

I couldn't run. Almost as if the old man had put metal pins through my bones and fastened me to the floor of which I stood on. But that is what happens in a nightmare.

He starts to unbutton his shirt, fiddling with the bottom button between his fingertips. The color of his skin is a lunchmeat grey; like the color of someone who has been buried six feet under. He begins to unbutton his pants, "This is what you came for. This is what I want," He whispers in my ear. He slowly removes his pants, one leg at a time as if I would expect anything different from this monster. As if this predator were to devour me with a fork and knife instead of using his teeth. I almost throw up, trying to hold back the vomit in my throat. Where his genitalia should be, nothing is there. No shriveled-up penis, nor clump of adulthood. But a grey bump, like a doll.

Now I understand why he'd stayed around town, collecting whatever knowledge of whatever he could about us, about our species. Whatever he was, he was morphing into us.

Stealing body parts from the local cemetery. Arms and legs and whatever else he could collect. Every day, he was becoming more human, one of us. Underneath his jacket is a carving knife; the kind of blade used to cook sliced meats, poultry, and fish or even hack off a few fingertips. Or extremities.

The old man orders me to take off my clothes. He rubs his crotch with the edge of the blade, saliva dripping out of the cavern in long thimble strands. I'm half asleep, tumbling around in a terrible dream that seems all too familiar. The second patch of yellow lighting paints a stroke into the midnight air, this one much louder than before which wakes the house-cat. It scurries across my feet to look back at me with prominent yellow eyelids.

I'll lift my head off the pillow, gasping for breath. I grip my arm. The old man is gone, but for the moment. My fingernails dig into my flesh and go deep, but I do not bleed like humans do.

I roll over. Putting a hand on top of the mushy lump next to me. "Sweetheart," I whisper, reaching over the lump with one hand. The lump stirs, repositioning itself back onto its side. I kick myself out of bed. The floorboards creak beneath my footsteps, on the way to our children's room. Both of our children are usually sound asleep. I turn the doorknob and peek into their chamber.

They are still, huddled under a mess of blankets. But for some reason, I must count for the both of them. Sometimes I will wake them up with a smile or talk to them for a bit. Just to know that they are still here. I'll be sure to count each finger or toe.

Do you see the each of them, sleeping so sound as their chests beat so soft? Beating up then down through a ribcage and an interconnected system of arteries and muscle and rich blood pumping through their veins so full.

I tiptoe downstairs to the kitchen and pour myself a tall, cold glass of water. It begins to rain outside, splattering against the window. A second gargantuan thunder rumble tumbles down from the sky, and I jump, backing up. The air feels thin, my lungs lunging for oxygen. I'll need a spacesuit or air-tank to walk around.

Tears slide out of both eyelids and down my cheeks. I pick up my feet, shuffling them back to my bedroom where I shut the door behind me and turn the lock.

I slip back into bed and lie still, like the dead. The lump turns around, peeling away the bed sheet like excess skin. The old man positions himself up against my chest. Cupping his head between my shoulders, like a warm blanket. The clump of yellow hair on his head wiggles around like tiny mealworms; freshly dug out of the wet earth after a rainstorm. His fingernails are long and dead. "Is something the matter, darling?" He gives me a peck on the cheek. His kiss is cruel and unusual. His animal grin is familiar.

Sort of like reality. But my dream is no longer with me. It is dead. Evaporating like steam in a hot bathhouse. Up, up, and out of my head.

"There was sweetheart, I think it was in a dream that I had. But it is nothing, just a memory from when I was a little boy." I whisper.

He purses his lips together. Seemingly interested. "Oh, what about." He retorts. "I do not remember. But I think that a hungry wolf was chasing me. I still hear the wolf's stomach rumble. But I got away, just in time." I grit. Looking up at the ceiling.

"That sounds absolutely terrifying. But remember, it is just a dream." He whispers in my ear. I look at him, managing a half smile. I try to shut both eyes. "Of course, sweetheart. Just a dream."

Wisdom

Can lightning strike twice? He didn't think so, not in this life. If you were lucky enough to be in the right place at the right time, then that was that. You had one shot. There was not much that you could do. You could be prepared, that was all you could bring to the table. You had to wait for the opportunity. The youth would never understand, he thought.

Everything had to be delivered on a platter, to their table. They were hungry, but couldn't wait for the food to cook. The orange sun is out this afternoon, shining its bright energy beams through the thick evergreen trees, and onto relaxed faces. A tiny squirrel grabs a large nut, scampering up a tree. Birds chirp to one another, singing their praise. The old man sits cross-legged, on a bench in the park.

Thinking to himself that he had never seen a brighter day. It was almost like the world owed the living something. He smiles as a couple of joggers' tread past him, one pushing a baby stroller. To them, he is no more of a problem then the birds in the trees.

That's what he was counting on.

There is a newspaper, rolled up on his lap. He opens it every time somebody passes by. If you were to look closely enough, one would see that the paper was dated one year ago. The old man is a great actor, pretending to read. While he watches the children play.

Across from his bench, is the playground. Children are hooting and hollering, with a bountiful zest for life. The parents stand nearby, either on their phones or with a look of relaxed boredom on their faces. Unaware. There is a shark in the water.

The old man grins like a hungry wolf, beneath a rubber façade of long cruel wrinkles and silver hair. Nobody ever suspects the sweet old man. He had gotten away with a lot. As a young man, he kept these delicate interests too himself. He had learned early on. Where society only pays attention to the exterior, one forgets about the depraved mind underneath. Who controls the machine.

The old man licks his lips, preparing for dinner.

The Duel

Well, here we go Abel.

I have a name but what does it matter when you're dead. A person is given a name to be identified, not to be buried alive with. Down here.

There is a gun on the table and no way out. A friend under dire circumstances. But the gun wasn't supposed to be for me, no. It was supposed to be for a coyote or two. It was supposed to keep me safe. Life's little ironies. I pick my friend up off the table and bite down on the barrel hard. "Just squeeze the trigger, Abel," I tell myself. But, I cannot.

What makes me human is precisely what keeps me down here in the bunker. The fear of what comes after. Is there a heaven or hell? If so, will I be a part of a duel between two sadists for my soul? Only God and Satan have the answers.

That and what is blocking the door. I can't do it. My back is covered in a slick, cold sweat, and my mouth is dry. It is not the right time to die, I lie to myself.

I scream my name as loud as I can. But nobody can hear me down here. That is a fact. But, it feels good to let everything out at once.

It took me two years to build the underground bunker. Spending time away from my family and whatever was expected of me in society. Down here. It felt great at first, like a drug. My mother and father had wanted me to be a doctor or lawyer. I needed a reality check. It was simple. Every Friday, after work, I would pack up my truck with a shovel, a pair of gloves, a jug of water and some bread, and drive out into the desert.

In the glove compartment, I kept a small pistol for the coyotes. I never had to use it.

The spot that I was going to dig my underground bunker was beneath a tall and handsome green tree. It was simple to find. I called it the miracle tree. The tree, a beautiful anomaly in a terrain of grey rock and rattlesnake, somehow had managed to grow. Defying science and logic. Just as I was defying societies expectations of me. This tree would give me a spot to rest underneath as I continue to work tiredly throughout the day.

This had to be the spot. God had truly blessed me. Or so I thought....

The morning before the storm came through, I had put a new door on the bunker. I decided to wait out the storm in the bunker, instead of driving into the city. Loud yellow thunder, coming down like a black bullwhip. Too close.

Outside of the bunker, I hear a crash. Something falls on top of the door making an indent in the metal frame.

I scramble up the steps frantically. A long vine with tattered leaves sticks through a crack in the door. The tree had fallen on top of the door. I push on the door with everything I have. Leaning my shoulder into it. No budge. Pounding on the door of my tomb with both fists.

A little while later after the storm clears, a single tumbleweed rolls across the highway. On its own, for miles and miles. Sometime later, I examine the rations left in the bunker. I had enough food and water for thirty days. So, it goes.

Well, this is it folks, your favorite part of the story. You don't have much time left when the metal barrel of the gun tastes better than the food.

Every morning, I crawl up to the top of the steps and pull a leaf or two off one of the branches jutting through the door. Crunching it with my boot. Should I be upset? Probably not, but I can't help it. There's not a lot I could do about it. There is a lesson that you must learn about life.

Abel lowers his voice to a whisper, as he also lowers the pistol. He sets in on the ground next to his leg. Brushing it with the tips of his bony fingers.

"Talking to myself again, I bet you think that's hilarious." He laughs, looking down at the pistol.

The pistol sits on the ground not saying a word.

"You did this didn't you, you beautiful bastard," Abel replies, winking at the pistol. "Huh-oh look at you. I have a date with death do I not. But you're the gracious matchmaker. Day thirty-three." He screams, pounding the floor.

Then he picks the gun up and puts his mouth around the barrel. Tears come down from his cheeks and onto the black handle. Closing both of his eyes. Abel sniffles once or twice, positioning himself on the ground in the curled fetal position facing towards the door of the bunker. He wraps a couple of fingers around the trigger…as his stomach begins to gargle, scooping whatever air is left inside his stomach and ringing it like a bell. One last supposed biological alert before he would succumb to this hunger.

Abel begins to laugh as his stomach growls one more time. A young man enters the steady descent into madness, which will prepare him for death. Abel couldn't help but hear the growling noise.

It sounded like…a coyote. The young man's stomach rumbles for the last time. Abel closes both of his eyes again, but cannot stop from laughing. He pictures the coyote howling at the moon.

The very creature he had brought the gun for. Now he had found one down here in the bunker with him. Inside him. He would take the creature with him down to hell.

"I gotcha buddy," Abel whispers, trying to keep a straight face as he pulls the trigger.

Woman

Two men stand side-by-side, unable to take their eyes off the woman.

She is the most beautiful woman that either had ever seen. Long thick black hair, down to her shoulders. Gorgeous Ocean blue eyes as enchanting as the deep itself.

One of the men sees the other looking at the woman. He laughs, patting him on the back. "In another life, my friend." He says. His friend turns around, shaking his head.

"A woman like that is priceless. She comes around once in a lifetime. You will get a tiny glimpse of her passing you by, and then she will fade into the oblivion. Never to be seen from again. Unaware of your existence, but you lust for hers. This life is unfair."

He grins a wolfish grin. "My friend, everybody has a price, it is just how much are you willing to pay."

He pulls back the sheet. His friend flips on the light in the mortuary. Both men stare at the body underneath the sheet. The dead woman on the table does not say much. The dead tend to be heavy sleepers.

"She was so beautiful, it is such a shame." His friend lowers his voice. He reaches into his jacket pocket, pulling out a wad of green bills. "How long will I get with her?" He continues, handing him the big wad of green.

The man takes the wad, handing his friend a set of jingling keys. "Well, my shift is over in about an hour. Don't forget to lock up when you are done."

He gives his friend another pat on the back. He turns around, his footsteps echoing down the hall.

His friend looks down at the dead woman and begins to unbuckle his pants.

Taking Lives

My father died with a knife stuck in his heart. The murderer had crawled in through the bedroom window, and back out after the deed had been done. I had thought about going after our killer, but I knew he was well and indeed gone. By now, I wouldn't doubt he had found a hiding spot. If there were a search, I would have to look behind every building and up every tree.

Besides, my father told me not to go after his murderer. He did fear for his life towards the end. "Somebody is coming after me, it won't be long now." He told me.

Underneath his eyes are black bags; I could tell he had not been sleeping. "Nobody is coming after you," I blurt. My face grew deep with worry.

"I have not been happy for a while my son, ever since your mother passed, things have been difficult. In many ways, I am a broken man, but life does this to us you see. Pretty soon I will be taken to see her."

I lean back in my chair, visibly shaken. "Who is going to take you, father?" He stares at me.

"The somebody who murdered your mother, he has come back to collect."

I gasp. "Father, stop it!"

He places his hand over mine. "I hope that you do not search for him, wasting your life, trying to find a reason. Instead, write your stories.

Live.

When he is gone, it is because he wants to be. For the moment."

I could not believe it. But I did as he had told me. About a week later, he took his own life. I went to his funeral. There is no talk of suicide. But only the glorious life he lived. He was buried next to my mother. I did not continue to search in any way.

So, I grew up, and I wrote my own stories. I became a doctor, just like my father. I met a beautiful girl, and grew a belly and lost my hair. I got older. My youth is gone, but I see bits and pieces of myself in our children.

I hang up a picture of my father and a picture of my mother above the fireplace. Both are smiling. I smile back.

Underneath the Skin

We are somebody we pretend to be. Every one of us has a dark secret that needs to be told. But to do so, we must dig underneath the skin. Peel away at the layers.

I am in love with another woman. Just don't tell my wife. This other woman means the world to me. She is my sunrise and sunset. Before I shut both eyes and rest my head on the pillow, I think of her before I dream.

You can tell a lot about someone if you spend time in his or her bedroom. Their entire life is on display, every vulnerability or secret.

A failing relationship has a lot in common with the life of a reptile. Reptiles, such as lizards or snakes, must be able to regulate their body temperatures by moving to different climates, such as a warm rock or a more heated channel of air. Or we begin to die.

Our marriage is on the rocks. My wife and I sleep in separate bedrooms. But she has faith in our relationship, that things will get better. If I were a better man, I would tell her about the other woman in my bed.

She is on the bed with her legs spread apart and a cigarette between her lips. "No, you wouldn't, we belong together," the woman whispers, rising off the bed like a venomous snake coming out of a basket.

She begins to unbutton her blouse, and then her bra. Hands them to me. "Put them on," The woman tells me. I nod my head, enthusiastically. She dumps her makeup bag on the bed, and I pick up a tin container of cherry red lipstick.

It takes me an hour or so to do her makeup and the eyeliner. Peeling back the layers. To adjust the platinum blonde wig and put on her heels. Slowly we become one. Later, she corrects herself, seeing a bit of who he used to be in the mirror.

"Ready, my darling." She whispers, using his lips.

He nods, looking back at her with the same two eyes.

The two go hand in hand out the door.

The Family

Family dinner with our son, our passion project, we joke. "He's growing up so fast," my wife beams. She's right. The two of us sit back in our chairs as adults, contemplating the cruelty of father time who eventually takes everything.

"Samuel has your hair and my eyes." She smiles, ruffling a hand through our child's mop of blonde hair. Samuel plays with a piece of cauliflower on his plate, silent. "Fortunately got my looks, eh" I grin. My wife lifts her head back, laughs.

"Sam; sweetheart, eat your vegetables." She taps his plate with the tip of her steak knife. Samuel bites his lip. "I want to go home."

My wife looks back at me, red. "You are home sweetheart, with us." Samuel turns pale, afraid. My wife picks up the knife and waves it at our boy. "You are not Samuel; my Sam would never speak back to his mother."

"Sweetheart, calm down." I blurt. "We didn't get it right, again. "—She's sobbing. "The hair bleach, he's even wearing Samuels clothes, but I don't see my son, only this boy. Please take him back. My wife collapses, dropping the knife. I'm angry at the indignation of life. Reality. "Our son is dead Beth, I don't know what else to do," I yell. My wife stumbles away, sobbing uncontrollably.

"Please mister, I'll say nothing. I want to go home." The boy sobs. I bury my face in both hands, cursing.

Why couldn't you have just played along kid, for the both of us? A voice hollers inside my head, the fantasy. This boy disgusts me. Instead, I lie. Like this family, everything I tell him is a lie.

I'll take him home tomorrow, and his family will be happy to see him. In the back of my truck are a shovel, two flashlights, and a bind of rope. He'll be buried in an unmarked grave next to the other "Samuels."

On to the next one. My wife wants a happy family again.

I won't stop till we are.

The Dragon

It's black outside and pissing rain. The house is just as dark, and the old man that I had come to kill is sound asleep. Unaware that somebody is in the house. I tiptoe across the hall and up the staircase, a hand on the barrister. Thunder cracks outside.

Most nightmares start this exact way. Right before the masked boogeyman arrives with a knife in his hand.

Mine is different. For me, there is no boogeyman; there is only a dragon. But I have learned to deal with my demons. I am the knight in shining armor, arriving on horseback. Ready to vanquish the dragon. The dragon, a two-cylinder, gas guzzling, metal death trap driven by the old man that snorts fire and burns rubber.

But tonight, the old man is human. His car is parked downstairs, and his blood is warm. I open the door to his bedroom after I reach the top of the staircase, taking a peep inside. He is asleep, and a woman is lying next to him. Lost in a dream world.

I must ask myself the question. How does a killer sleep so softly?

When I close both of my eyes to go to sleep at night, I'm eleven years old again. It's a bright blue summer afternoon. I'm playing out on the gravel driveway in front of my home with a friend. My friend shoots the basketball, sticking his tongue out just like Michael Jordan. The ball bounces off the backboard, rolling off the driveway and into the street.

The Dragon comes around the corner, stopping just in time. As the basketball rolls on under its belly. Swallowing it whole. The car sits still on the road, humming a soft beat through the engine. I look over at my friend. Both of us can see the orange basketball, jammed underneath.

We walk over to the car. The drivers' side window rolls down, and the palest man I had ever seen in my life stick his head out. Ghostly. His eyes are beet red. Like he was allergic to the outside air.

"Did one of you boys throw a ball at my car?" There is a frown on his face.

"No—sir," My friend stammers. Explaining the story. He points underneath the car.

"Is that--…so," Pale man, says. - "Well, let me move--," -But my friend interrupts- "Wait! You'll crush the ball, mister..." He points, underneath the car. The pale man stares at both of us, uninterested. We hear the dragon shift back into first.

"Wait! I ca–n get the ball, its right there," My friend looks over at me, desperate. I look up and down the empty street. We are alone. "It's just a ball," I whisper, grabbing his arm. "Let's go back inside. He doesn't care". I grit. The engine continues to hum.

"Get your ball kid. I got the car in park," Pale man starts to roll the window up.

My friend drops to his knees, crawling beside the car. "Hold up, I got it." He murmurs. Sliding an arm underneath the car. The window stops. The pale man snaps, sitting back in his seat. I bite my lip. "Well, go on...I guess," I tell my friend. My friend nods his head. Getting on his stomach, going underneath the car to reach for the ball. "Erre-we goooo!" My friend shouts, scooping the ball with his fingertips.

The pale man whispers to himself, grinning mischievously. I only catch the last part, just as he rolls the window up, disappearing behind a dark screen. A soft subtle, "Bye, bye birdie."

Click. The car, shifts into first. "No!" I shout, reaching down to grab my friends leg, sticking out. "Got it!" my friend snickers, at the same time. The car shoots forward, jumping over my friend, the human speed bump. A gush of blood splatters over my face and chest like a burst water balloon. The dragon roars, taking off around the corner and out of the neighborhood.

Screaming, I stumble across the road to a neighbor's house. Half blind and stupid. Banging on the front door. This part is more or less a blur. A glitch in time. Everything seems to work in slow motion. My ears are ringing. In the nightmare, somebody usually answers their door, looks down at me, and joins me in my terrified efforts. A half blind, bloody boy, pulling on their pants leg.

It's the same dream, like every other night. Nothing much has changed over the past twenty years. I always wake up in reality. The real nightmare.

Upstairs in the bedroom, I had tied up the dragon and his wife. Both struggle with their binds and the duct tape around their mouth. I rip the duct tape off the old man's mouth, showing him the knife. "If you scream, I'll kill her in front of you," I whisper. I put the knife under the dragons' throat. Looking into his terrified eyes.

"You look different, but then, after twenty years, so do most. You got a spray tan, and you put on a few pounds, but I know it's you," I grit my teeth, pushing the blade under his Adam's apple. "Your eyes are still the same color, I could never forget them. Not in my wildest dreams or nightmares. Because you are my nightmare." The old man mumbles, looking over at his wife. I hold his head still.

"That wasn't the first time, no, there were three other instances. When you first met me, you had done it once before. But, the last one eventually brought me here too you. You got sloppy. There was someone who got a description as you were driving away." I hoist the old man up, pushing him out the bedroom door. His wife screams, flopping around on the floor. He turns around, "Everything's going to be alright, Marla!" I push him forward. "Downstairs, we are going for a little drive."

Downstairs. The garage. I tell him to get the keys. There are two cars, parked in the garage, and both under thick tarps. Using the same hand, I peel the tarp off the closest car. Throwing it onto the ground. My heart, pounding in my chest. Needing to come out. Recognizing the other monster. I lean over and kiss the hood of the car. "The hunt is over." I run my hand alongside the back of the car. "You change the license plate after each murder, and you give it a different color," I look at him. "But this is the one. I know who you are; you wouldn't use another car. This was your child."

The old man just stares at me, a perplexed look

on his face, which slowly turns into a tight grin. In the shallow light, I can see him now. In his full form. Somehow, the tan is gone. He stands before me, with a pale complexion, and big dark round orbs for both eyes. That could see through walls. He runs a hand alongside the car.

"Whatever you're going to do with me, don't hurt her," He whispers. I open the passenger side door. "Get in."

When he turns around to get in, I get behind him, bringing the knife up under his throat. Blood spills all over the passenger seat. He reaches for the opening in his throat, gargling. I push him onto the seat and close the door. I come to the drivers' side door and get in. He's already dead; by the time I put the key in the ignition. "Bye, bye, birdie," I whisper as the garage door opens, letting the outside rain spill inside. It mixes in with the blood, washing it away like the incoming tide.

I pull the dragon out onto the city street with the dead man in the passenger seat, on a destination set for nowhere. To a place hotter than hell, or perhaps, until I'd long forgotten the memory of that warm summer afternoon. So long ago.

However long that takes.

Rainy Season

Have you ever watched a couple of children play in the rain? When I was a child, my mother used to lock me out until dinnertime. You get used to it. Somebody else's terrible weather is usually my favorite. I caught a lot of colds as a kid, but I was taught enough. I was not raised by a set of parents. If you pay close enough attention, Mother Nature is a fantastic babysitter. The weather and I were partners in crime. The hot summertime heat is excellent for swimming and the winter is for throwing giant snowballs with friends. However, the rainy season is and will always be, my favorite.

Someone once asked me if I believe in God. No, I believe in the weather. This was right after I told them I was going to murder them and that I would get away with it.

"You have a good soul, Jesus teaches us too love one another, what had I ever done to you," the person cries after I tell him to get on his knees. Pray.

I place the knife to his throat. The wind picks up, ruffling the top part of my coat. "God is listening. He obviously wants you dead," I whisper. It begins to rain outside as the dark clouds build up, overhead. Plummeting towards the earth in Hiroshima style bombs. I stick out my tongue, like a child tasting sweet cotton candy. Yellow thunder cracks in the tall sky like a bullwhip.

When I was little, I would run and hide underneath the bed covers when the storm came. Now, it is my opportunity. With a single thrust, I slide the blade across his throat.

Thunder. "If you can hear me, wash away my sins," I scream; tossing my head up into the air. I drop the knife onto the city street. Clang. In less than half an hour, a rush of water will float the knife down into the storm drain. My bloody hands will be squeaky clean. Crucial evidence washed away. I look up at the sky, a grin on my face

"Thank you, partner.

What I Need

Love is like tumbling out of a window. The fall is much harder than the impact. His breath is icy cold as if he were delivering the verdict at a murder trial. I can feel it on the back of my neck. "Come here, darling, and put your head on my chest," He whispers, collecting a fistful of my hair. Our lovemaking is wild and exotic upon the midnight hour, we purge. Both of us lost in a kaleidoscope of flesh.

Afterwards, we lie next to one another, my ear pressed on his chest. Thump. Goes his big red heart. "You love me, don't you" I tug on his arm. Our touch is frigid.

I find the courage to ask him another question. "Am I ever going to see you again," pours out of my lips, like salmon swimming upstream.

My lover looks at me for a long moment, then digs into the left pocket of his coat and pulls out a small silver ring. Sliding it onto his finger. "I'm afraid that I have a prior engagement, but we'll be in touch." He says, pushing past me.

I begin crying. "You are what I need," I plead. He looks at me, shaking his head. As if I was supposed to understand what this was, all along.

Somehow, I manage to get up and out of bed, every morning after. My nights are restless, and my head is a solar system of thought. I can do nothing but think of him, for he fills me up, like a giant meal. Nourishing a broken heart. But eventually, we tell ourselves to move on.

One evening, I wake up in considerable pain. "Get out of me, I no longer need you," I scream, thrashing about. Clenching my stomach. I crawl alongside the floor until I get to the bathroom. In the bathroom sink, is the bloody knife that I had shown him. Tears cascade down both cheeks, but I wipe them away. Thump. His heart and my heart beat next to one another.

But, I couldn't take him with me. So I had to consume whatever I could.

I open the toilet seat and lean over the bowl. Retching. When I open both of my eyes, there are a couple bloody bits and pieces of him that I had consumed, including a finger dancing in the toilet water. The rest of him I had been unable to eat.

"You were what I needed," I whisper.

Monsters

The man opens his eyes, exhaling and covered in perspiration, his torso dripping an icy cool. It is dark, and he clutches his beating heart. Excitement. He sits straight up, slipping his legs from under the sheet and onto the cold floor. For the last hour, he has pretended to be asleep. The woman sleeping next to him continues with her dream, foregoing any responsibility for a later date.

He had paid her good money to spend the night. She had listened to him talk about his wife and children that he missed. "Separation is a bitch," he told her. That was the first lie. Both were dead. He would never be seeing either of them again. The second lie; which was a truth, was the one that he told the psychologist during the murder trial, that the monsters under his bed were not real, that they weren't responsible for the murders, but the ones in his head are.

That one had gotten him six months in the psychiatry ward instead of death row. The man smiles a wolfish grin, saliva dripping from his lips. He reaches his hand under the bed, pulling out the fireman's axe he had left there. The monster under the bed. He grasps the wooden handle between his two hands, looking at himself through the silver reflection of the blade. "Without me, you're powerless," he whispers, kissing the axe.

Then, he straddles her with the axe in one hand raised above his head. He clamps the other down over her mouth. The woman opens both of her eyes, trying to scream.

"No matter what your parents told you, monsters are real, and ghosts are real too." He whispers. "They don't live under the bed, waiting till you turn the light off or go to sleep. They also aren't hidden behind your closet door, either. They live inside us, and sometimes, they win."

He brings the axe down.

The Couple

Both agreed that a great relationship is built on trust. Andrea could trust Andrew with any secret, no matter how extravagant, and it would only strengthen their relationship. "I want to be you're very last," She whispers in his ear. "There were other girls, before. But now, everything that you had is before. I want to consume you. Remember nothing of what was, only what you have now and forever," Andrew just stares at her, with pregnant eyes. Never surer of his love for another human being. She could tell, he didn't have to say anything back.

She gets on top and begins to ride him. Their lovemaking is like a scene from a movie.

He is sweet, tall, and gentle. He lets her do all the work. Andrea is fiery, enigmatic, and lively. A bunch of wild horses galloping across the plain. Both contrast each other perfectly. Night and day. The living and the dead.

Andrea steps out of the dead man's casket, and onto the marble floor. She adjusts herself, smoothing the hem of her dress with both palms. She turns around. There are people pointing fingers at her or screaming her name. Everyone at the funeral is clad in black, like the reaper, and their complexions tomato red. Somebody teeters back and forth, before vomiting into the aisle. An elderly woman begins to shriek, leaping up from her seat. She stumbles in the vomit and comes crashing down, sending her silver cane flying through the air.

A couple of policemen push through the massive cathedral doors, just as Andrea tries to make a run for it. Hands go around her body, tugging her to the floor.

The Murder

"Would you murder someone, anyone, if knew that you would never be caught?" my friend Robert asks me. I shrug my shoulders. "I don't know."

Robert crosses his arms. "Why not?" he says. "How can I be completely one-hundred percent sure that I wouldn't get caught," I reply. "Everybody thinks that their not going to be caught, but still go through with it." Robert bites his lip.

I lean over, positioning myself over our campfire. I glance up at the stars.

"Let's forget right and wrong; that's out the window. So, you would risk everything, just to murder someone?" Our fire flickers an orange ember and the pine trees dance in the wind.

"It's like if you wanted a person dead so bad; that you would be willing to carry them miles to nowhere, just to thrust that dagger into their gut! If you feel like that, there's nothing stopping you." Robert nods his head.

I rub my hands together over the fire. "So, murderers do it for themselves, to quench whatever hate is inside. It wouldn't matter if they got caught." Robert looks down. "Then the whole question is irrelevant, isn't it?" We both sit in silence.

"Your right lets do it." I exhale, the thoughts circulating in my head like a slow ceiling fan. "We're actually going through with this. Fuck. I need this, though."

The man that we had kidnapped and tied up struggles with his binds; rolling over in the dirt. Nearby to the campfire is our truck. Sitting next to the truck are two shovels and leftover rope.

Robert nods, looking at the knife in his hands. Both of us go and kneel beside the man. "Nobody will ever find him out here, we did well," Robert exhales, looking at me nervously. I agree. "We'll bury him together."

I grip the top half of the handle; Robert grips the lower half. We steady it above his heart.

On the count of three, we thrust down.

THE PIPE

(the end of the road)

I suppose the grim reaper comes in the form of a plumber if you think about it. Here to unclog you and all the sick, the elderly, the accidents, the suicides, and all the professional daredevils from the system. What's that? You spot a single sliver of grey hair or an irregular heartbeat that ticks in your chest like a time bomb.

You're getting older, aren't you? Day by day, bit by bit, until you begin to crumble into the dust. He sees that, and it makes him smile.

The Plumber smacks his lips before setting his tool bag down on the ground, and then pulls out a pair of stained leather gloves and a dirty rag from his pocket.

The plumber lowers the rag over your nostrils, your body twitching back and forth. A head beats against the floor, one thump, and two thumps. Your body lies still. Blood drips from both ears.

The plumber works quietly, dragging your body through your home and into the long cast iron tub in your bathroom. He turns on the water.

Warm water hits the side of your head, draining the blood from the hole in your head into an drain that collects into a froth of brains and pulp and beauty. There is no need for the healthy to exist with the dead.

A world extinguished in one instant, and all fear,

ambition, and dreams are known to be–

Flushed awayyyyyyyy—down where shit and sin are disposed of and taken to an underbelly of our beautiful world.

Drip. Drip, he washes you off, cleaning your corpse of all its many years of disgusting sins of human waste, neglect, and lifestyle down the drain. All gone now.

The shit is pushed out the other side where there have been rumors of golden harps, or legendary bass players and your grandma is swimming in a cold and dark river although she has no sense of the feeling. It smells rancid as the stew mixes into one common sickness pissing in from above.

Others whom you have met before and whom you would have introduced yourself to swim with you now all in the same pond of bullshit. A human race collective stew is well prepared; from the good to the bad; religious to atheist; from murderers to the straight edge; from pedophiles to parents. All collected in the same vat, everyone is here.

The suicide bomber disguised as the substitute teacher from Sudan with twelve pounds of C4 strapped to the inside of his jacket pisses out in front of you with the school bus full of twelve-year-old's that he hijacked early this morning spewing out close behind; pissing out from the drain.

A middle-aged mother dying of cancer takes her life in Santa Barbara California, slitting her wrists in a bathroom comes out next raining down like a morning shower as the reaper smiles with an umbrella in its right hand, dragging another corpse into the bathtub.

Drip. Drip. All the same froth, a mixture of bone, innards, and blood.

A twenty-one-year-old woman decides to go skydiving with her boyfriend. Her parachute fails to open somewhere in Wisconsin, and her body is not discovered for two days, dragged to the nearby woods by two hungry wolves with yellow eyes.

The neighbor from across a familiar street, the one you've known for quite some time, is tragically hit by a Red Chevrolet on his way to work, his body folding backward like a spring.

There goes a handsome minister from Maine, swallowing a box of pills.

Do you see that? An elderly woman with eight grandchildren surrounds her hospital bed somewhere in Berlin, a family affair. They all pray for her as she shuts those eyes for the last time.

Drip. Drip. Drip.

The pipe pours them & us into the sewer. Down here, we all float together. Let's drift along forever. The river continues to flow collecting higher and higher, but there is no roof. Look up as we go around this bend, voices squealing and nails scratching like children at a waterpark.

Splash.

A boy of thirteen wishes he hadn't overdosed on LSD and decided to jump off a building.

A local newspaper writer recites this young man's obituary, finishing with, "He is in a better place."

Parents weep, friends curse the heavens if it existed, relatives shed a tear for this young boy.

Drip. Drip.

There is no roof as the river continues to fill before overflowing and spilling out into an ocean of souls. Man, women, woman, man, woman, man, woman ride the wave and collect with all the others until we start to sink together. A river hisses and boils and steams and belches entombing the dead in this murky afterlife.

All-the-while—

A plumber slips his pants up with a thumb and tugs on his low-brim hat before picking up the tool-bag. He shuts your front door with a closed palm. His legs strut across the paved driveway and out into the street where he stops to open the driver's door of a black van parked beside a telephone pole; slinging the leather gloves across the passenger seat.

He'll whip the cap off and brush away the warm sweat that runs across his face, turn towards you with a sharp grin and a heavy growl;

"It's a dirty job, but someone's got to do it." For this is a regular workday for the reaper and a nine-five that never seems to end as the world continues to choke on our growing obesity; pulling us further into the murk.

Zoo

A group of people stand in front a large glass window at the zoo. Above the window is a sign that reads, exhibit. On the other side of the glass are a couple of large reptilians; crocodiles with long smiles.

A little girl from the group walks up to the window and places her palm on the glass. In the other hand is a brown teddy bear that she keeps close to her heart.

"Sweetheart, don't touch the glass." Her father moves over, grabbing her by the wrist. His face flushed white. A couple of the crocodiles look over at her with a pair of yellow eyes and then snap their jaws.

One of them moves up to the exhibit window, pushing its belly alongside the floor.

Then it did something else entirely.

The crocodile had to be every bit of seven feet tall when it stood on its hind legs, straightening itself up against the window. It had a long neck and a long tail that wagged back and forth like a puppy dog.

But when it turns around, eyeing the small group, it is grinning from ear to ear.

The girls face is pale, and her heart pounds in her chest like a drum. This was much scarier than any night terror she had ever had.

A couple of people in the group begin to scream.

The crocodile shakes its head and begins to laugh with them, erupting a medieval roar from the pit of its belly.

"Look how small you are." It grins, turning its head around. "Alec, come here. Look at the girl. She is adorable." It retorts. The croc waggles a sharp-toothed claw towards its friends.

A couple of the other crocs stand up and approach the window. One of them has a straw hat on its head and a tight button up shirt that fits snug on its shoulders.

The other has a disposable camera in front of its face. The crocodile presses down on the top button, and the camera gives out a white flash.

"No flash photography, please!" One of the crocodiles' yells. This one has a pair of spectacles that sit on the end of its snout and a small clipboard in one claw.

It walks up to the window and turns around, facing the other reptiles.

"Ladies and gentlemen, this part of the tour is my favorite. Here at our facility, we pride ourselves on our most extensive collection of rare animals in the world.

Homo Sapiens were believed to be a significant percentage of the world at one time. Or "Human," which is the common name given to any individual of the species, were believed to have first evolved at least two point three to two point five million years ago." It finishes, offering a broad smile.

One of the other crocs from the group speaks up. It talks with a thick country accent as if it were stirring the words in a pot and scooping them out with a spoon. "Dem-, look likes- a bunch of apes that I saw on the television set." It grins, thumbing a soft collection of laughter from the audience.

The croc at the head of the group nods its head. Adjusting the pair of spectacles on its nose in the process.

"Yes, you would be correct sir. In fact, the closest living relatives of the homo sapiens are the gorilla and chimpanzee." It smiles. "Which is a great transition to our next exhibit. Who would like to see a gorilla?" The croc points towards a door.

It leads the group into another room amidst an earful of chitchat and heavy footsteps.

The door closes, leaving a couple of the people behind the exhibit glass to sink onto their knees. Some bow down in prayer, while one rolls over onto her side facing the corner wall. It would be quiet without the sobbing.

The little girl holds her stuffed bear. Her father places a hand on her back, before giving his daughter a fake smile. "Everything is going to be all-right sweetheart." He whispers, digging the lie out through his lips.

Ordinary Monster

Sarah and Michelle lived together in a two-bedroom apartment just outside of the city.

Sarah is a receptionist at a high-powered law firm and just as equally as beautiful as the title would suggest. Her eyes are the color of the ocean and her lips a marvelous cherry red.

She was the type of girl another girl would be jealous over. Sarah had what everybody wants, everyone's attention.

Michelle was the polar opposite. Born shy and quiet with a streak of reclusiveness, the girl hadn't had a proper date in over a year.

Also, unlike Sarah, Michelle's eyes did not sparkle in the sun, and her complexion was not far from lunchmeat in the refrigerator.

There was nothing unusually striking about her. When Michelle stood next to her friend, she was nothing but an ordinary monster. The girl thought she ought to be removed like a virus.

Michelle hated Sarah in every way that she was not, but she also loved Sarah more than anybody in the world. She couldn't help but wonder what it would be like to be that beautiful. Michelle would dream about it.

Tonight, is no different. Just the beginning of a dream. Both girls are slightly intoxicated. An empty bottle of red wine is on the table in front of them, and the television is in the lounge room.

The girls had decided to stay in. Both had busy workweeks behind and ahead of them.

Michelle leans across the table and smiles. "You are beautiful; and the luckiest woman in the world. Tell me, Sarah, what is it like for people to flock to you." Her cheeks are a rosy red that matches the color of the wine.

Sarah giggles, biting her bottom lip. The girl flickers her finger, offering Michelle to come closer. "I don't think it matters my love." Sarah kisses her, pushing her tongue into her mouth.

The two girls cling to one another for a long moment. Until Michelle opens her eyes, pushing Sarah away. Gasping for breath. "What was that?" She exhales.

Sarah throws herself onto Michelle, wrapping her arms around her. "I have always been in love with you." She stutters, slurring her words.

"Since when!" Michelle gasps, backing up. "Since I was done with men obviously!" Sarah replies, beginning to cry.

"Wha—how, could you! I have dreamed of being you." Michelle mumbles, shaking her head. But Sarah pounds her hands on the floor. "You should see the way men look at me. Like I am a prize at the state fair. A piece of meat on two legs with a pair of breasts and lips!" She screams, shedding more tears.

"You are drunk, that is all…." Michelle whispers.

"But you are everything that I am not, and I love you for it. Say that you love me too." Sarah cries, holding her friend's hands.

But Michelle waves her head. "I-I don't!" Michelle hollers, screaming at the top of her lungs. Sarah covers her face with both hands.

Michelle retreats, stumbling out of the lounge room and back to her room, slamming the door shut.

Michelle sits back against the door, eyes red and puffy. Back out in the lounge room Sarah sobs uncontrollably.

In the morning, Michelle rolls out of bed, peeking her bedroom door open a tad. The lounge room and hallway are empty. She wipes the sleep from her eyes and tiptoes into the kitchen.

"Michelle I'm sorry." A soft voice whispers behind her. Michelle pivots around. Sarah gives her a more delicate smile, one foot crossed over the other. Only something is different this morning.

Michelle's face morphs into an upside-down smile, forcefully etched across her cheek like a lousy sculptor driving his chisel into a marble statue.

"Sarah, what did you do!"? She cries.

"I feel better my love." Sarah giggles. Sarah was bald; all her beautiful long hair had been cut off, and both of her eyebrows were gone.

Michelle was sure that if she were to use the bathroom, she would find bits of hair in the sink and an electric razor is dangling from its cord over the toilet.

Sarah had also gone through her familiar makeup routine but smeared her cherry red lipstick across her face and cheek.

The girl looked like a circus clown in the pouring rain. Hideous. Terrifying even.

Michelle nearly collapses, grabbing a side of the sink for leverage.

"I did a lot of thinking last night. No man will look at me the same again. I want to be invisible for a while. Nobody will ask me for a number ever again as long as I live. I also quit my job this morning. Everything that I hated about my life is over." Sarah smiles triumphantly.

"No, No-Sarah!" Michelle shakes her head.

"I want to be an ordinary monster just like you," Sarah whispers. Michelle holds her tongue, unable to speak.

Sarah moves on past her, opening the refrigerator door. She reaches inside and brings out a small plate covered in a shiny tin foil wrapper. Sarah takes the foil off and sets a giant apple pie on the kitchen counter, then opens a drawer and takes out a metal fork.

"I can eat whatever I want. Whenever I want. Desert for breakfast. Maybe I'll put on ten or twenty pounds, who knows!" Sarah digs into the pie, getting herself a small slice.

She then proceeds to lick some leftover cream off the end of the fork.

"I'm-going to get ready for work, okay." Michelle stumbles. Her friend belches, scooping a bit of berry from her lip into her mouth. "Are you going to be okay?" Michelle finishes, scratching her head.

Sarah ignores her, her body further into the refrigerator. "O-k…" Michelle mumbles, exiting the kitchen.

Michelle gets ready for work as quickly as possible. When she is about to leave she opens the bedroom window and crawls out, stumbling to the car. Her heart racing.

Michelle gets off work at six o'clock, and her focus is on the constant buzz of traffic. It's Friday, and half of the population is on its way back from work, either for a drink or smoke. Or the beach sounded nice. Whatever wasn't work.

Her phone vibrates in her purse. A text message. She picks up the phone. It's Sarah.

"So, I think we should go out tonight. You?"

Michelle puts the phone down. She hadn't forgotten about her housemate, even though she had tried.

When she gets home, Sarah is on the couch with a bowl of vanilla ice cream. She turns around, half-smiling. "Hello sis," She retorts. Blowing her a kiss.

"Um-Sarah, are you ok?" Michelle bites her lip. Sarah puts the bowl of ice cream down. "I've never felt better in my life; did you get my text earlier?"

Michelle nods. "I don't know if you should be out in public right now. I think you should take it easy."

Her friend stomps her foot. "This is the happiest that I have been. You're going to take it away from me?"

Michelle lowers her head. "Ok, just one drink. But I think that you should talk to someone." Sarah smiles, giving her friend a tight bear hug.

"Everything is going to be just fine." She whispers in her friend's ear. A cold shiver runs up Michelle's spine.

In a couple of hours, the girls decide to get ready. Michelle does her hair, applies her makeup, and puts on her heels. Sarah finishes another pint of ice cream.

The girls decide to visit a nearby bar. Sarah orders the Uber; it arrives, dropping them off in front of the bar.

Michelle gets out of the car behind Sarah. She looks around, trying to avoid particular faces. Her friend walks up to the bouncer and smiles, flashing her I.D.

He gives her a long hard look. He hands the I.D back to her and looks at her friend, Michelle. "Is everything alright miss." He questions her.

Michelle bites her lip. "We are just out getting a drink, what is so wrong with that." The bouncer shakes his head. Sarah walks past him and into the bar. The bouncer grabs Michelle's arm, pulling her close.

"Listen girlie, no drugs in the bar, is that clear." Michelle nods her head, shaking off the bouncer. "Screw off," She spits, stumbling into the bar. The adrenaline bursting in her chest. When was the last time she had told somebody to do that? Never.

Michelle and Sarah find a seat at the bar. The bartender gives both of them a double take, scratching his head. Across the bar, circles of people begin to whisper their way.

Michelle gets up, excusing herself. Sarah turns around. "Where are you going?" She asks, grabbing her drink. "I-need-to use the bathroom." Scurrying off.

Michelle walks to the back of the bar, wiping away a tear from her eye. "Excuse me," Somebody whispers, tapping her on the shoulder. Michelle rubs her nose. The young man was staring back at her smiles, scratching the back of his head.

He is tall, at least six-one or two. With light blue eyes and messy brown hair. Probably around her age. Definitely cute. Michelle smiles, backing up against the wall.

"Are you here with the girl at the bar?" He asks; there is a beer in his other hand. Michelle shakes her head. "The bald girl? She is-uh-my roommate." She bites her tongue.

Cute Guy nods his head, taking a sip of the beer. "Cool. Cool." Michelle blushes, positioning one leg behind the other. "Yea...I-uh." She stumbles. Forgetting that she had to pee.

He grins, leaning over to whisper in her ear. "I saw you two at the bar talking; you're obviously the beautiful one. I couldn't keep my eyes off you."

Michelle takes a step back. She thought about everything she hated about her body. Nobody had ever complimented her before. Especially when she went out with Sarah. Usually, the men would go to her.

Michelle didn't have to pee anymore. Cutie takes her hand and the two walk over to the bar. Michelle can see her friend at the other end of the bar. She has a drink in her hand and a couple of seats to herself on either side. Which was odd considering how packed the bar was.

Michelle ducks her head down, pretending to fix her shoe. "What are you doing?" The Cute Guy laughs, leaning his head down to meet her.

Michelle turns a shade red, shaking her head. Only shrugging her shoulders. Cute Guy smiles, raising his hand towards the bartender.

He orders the two of them a round of drinks. "So, what is your name sweetheart?" He smiles, taking a sip of his beer.

"Michelle…" She responds, trying not to look him in the eye. Did she look awkward? She didn't think so.

"Michelle, nice to meet you. I am Brian." Cute Guy leans toward her, resting on one arm.

Michelle nods her head, looking across the bar. Sarah is still sitting by herself, with one hand around a beer.

Brian turns around, thumbing towards Sarah. "Is everything alright with you two." He whispers, lowering his voice.

"She is having some trouble…I thought it would be good for her to go out." Michelle says, taking a sip of her drink.

"You have a good heart for such a beautiful woman," Brian replies. Raising his beer. Michelle blushes, tapping the end of her drink on his instinctively. "Cheers…" She half-whispers. Biting her tongue on the last syllable. Oh god, that was so stupid, she thought.

Brian laughs, slapping the table. He then shrugs both shoulders, emptying the beer. "Another round?" He smirks, sliding both eyes from up her bosom where he meets her face to face.

Michelle covers a laugh, shaking her head in favor. She stares down at the empty bottle between her hands. The room begins to tilt and dance with her ongoing smile.

A couple of drinks later Michelle and Brian stumble out the front door of the bar, one arm on top another. Brian kisses her on the cheek; she tastes his cologne, feels his grips tighten around her waist.

Michelle wants to be lead and loved. Her body aches from her toes to her groin. But somehow, she manages to pull away.

Gasping for breath between breaths. The girl knew that she loved him. She loved him more than she loved herself because the magic potion of alcohol had told her so.

But that was not it. It couldn't be that simple. Michelle plants her lips on his lips and then pulls away.

Brian tasted so good. But so, do most boys that she was attracted to. It was the way he lingered with her, first at the bar, and then now out here. Michelle likened the feeling of being wanted to ecstasy.

The girl couldn't get enough, her body told her so. But her mind was apprehensive; it had set up too many barriers in the past.

She pushes away from Brian, shaking her head. "I need to find my friend." She stutters, half smiling. "She's over there." Brian curls his lip, pointing over in the corner of the bar.

Michelle turns around. Sarah is leaning against the wall with a cigarette in one hand. She brings the ciggy up to her mouth and inhales, then exhales the smoke through both nostrils.

Michelle gives Brian a soft smile, stumbling over to her friend. "Hey-Sarah." She waves, taking a drunken one-two step.

Sarah drops the ciggy, mashing it under her heel.

"He's cute, where did you pick him up," Sarah whispers, controlling an emerging smile.

"Stop-he'll hear you!" Michelle laughs, nearly falling onto her friend.

"Well, I could have given you much better," Sarah, replies, flicking her tongue in her friend's ear.

Michelle takes a step back, seemingly ducking and diving out of her drunkard state. Sarah laughs.

"I'm only joking Michelle. If you came out here to play with these insects, then I'll support you. But I'll also be the bug spray." She snorts, wrapping an arm around her friend.

The two girls wobble back to the front of the bar. Brian is standing with both hands in his pockets.

There is a black car parked on the curb with an Uber sticker on the windshield.

"I got you a ride home sweetheart." Brian smiles, kissing Michelle on the forehead. She blushes. He opens the back door, offering the two girls into the backseat.

Sarah looks over and shrugs her shoulders, hopping into the backseat.

"Take care of your friend. It cannot be easy being friends with the most beautiful girl in the room. "Brian leans over, massaging his tongue on Michelle's earlobe.

Michelle turns bright red trying to control herself. "Me." She stutters, hardly believing a word. Brian kisses her again, this time on the cheek. "Goodnight Michelle." He smiles. Shutting the door.

When the girls are dropped off at home, Sarah takes off both of her shoes and dives headfirst on the couch. Michelle looks on past her, her eyes vacant and her thoughts a set of scattered clouds in the sky.

"Cat got your tongue." Sarah smiles, stretching out her limbs.

"I think I'm a little drunk." Michelle stutters.

"A little love drunk, I can see it in the face. You're adorable." Sarah laughs, clapping her hands.

"Do you think he liked me?" Michelle wobbles. Looking at her friend.

"He adored you. That boy had the look of a wolf who hadn't eaten in a week." Sarah snickers, crossing both of her arms.

Michelle nods her head, stumbling towards the bathroom.

She shuts the door and balances herself on the sink. The girl looks up in the bathroom mirror. Her hair is a little messy and her face a pale moon.

Michelle stares at herself for a minute. She traces the outline of her face with a couple of fingers. Then she begins to smile. The smile forms slowly at first like a world pandemic, before spreading across her cheeks. Michelle feels an electric jolt run from her brain till the tip of her toes.

Brian and his words run through her head.

"It can not be easy being friends with the most beautiful girl in the room."

In the morning, there is a faint knock on the door.

Michelle gets out of bed and answers. Sarah is standing at the door with a smile on her face. "I thought we would get some breakfast, darling." She whispers. Her voice mellow and chill.

Michelle scratches her head. Her friend is wearing an old shirt and a pair of sweatpants with deep stains. She looked terrible, like a spider that had built a nest during a hurricane.

"I'm waiting, get ready, Michelle." She kisses her roommate on the cheek.

Michelle closes the door and rubs her temples. She looks at herself in the mirror and slumps her shoulders.

God, she didn't want to go with Sara. She didn't want to do much of anything with her bald friend, to be honest.

Michelle sighs. Closing her eyes. She sees him again.

"I had a dream about you, Brian. That you told me you loved me. No boy had ever done that before." She whispers to herself.

She hears the television flick on in the living room. Her housemate was watching cartoons.

"You have to feel some way about yourself," Michelle tells her reflection in the mirror. Observing every wrinkle or smudge in her complexion.

"What, that you're hideous. That he only talked to you out of sympathy." Michelle in the mirror mimics, laughing steadily.

Michelle takes a step back, shaking her head. The image in the mirror is back to normal again. "No, no, no." She whispers. Straightening both shoulders. You cannot think like that.

Brian's words from last night run through her head. The most beautiful girl in the room. Michelle smiles weakly to herself. "Then act like it." She murmurs, widening her smile.

She opens her bedroom door with a towel in one hand. The television is still on, and she can hear Sarah giggling along with the program.

Michelle tiptoes across the hall to the bathroom. She closes the door behind her. Then she bends over and opens one of the bathroom cabinets.

"Please, please be here," Michelle whispers. In the bottom cabinet is a small black bag. Michelle bites her lip and picks the bag up. Sarah hadn't thrown her makeup bag away.

She unzips the makeup bag and pulls out a silver tube of lipstick. She takes off the cap and slowly twists the handle. "This is crazy," she thought. Then she laughs. Michelle puts the tube back in the bag and turns around, opening the shower door.

She showers and then dries herself off. Tying her hair back into a tight bun. Michelle dumps the contents of the bag into the sink, ruffling through whatever she could identify.

It takes her a while to put on the lipstick, foundation, blush, mascara, and eyeshadow. Like an artist molding his magnum opus. She delicately applies the essentials.

When she is done, Michelle pops open a small compact mirror the size of a beetle and purses her lips together.

Her eyes go wide. "I look… good today," she thought. She had never said that out loud before. Michelle smiles.

She puts the bag under her arm, before shutting the bathroom door behind her.

"Darling, why are you taking so long" Sarah turns the television down.

"Um, just needed to get ready. I'll be out in a sec." Michelle stops. One hand on the doorknob.

In her bedroom, she shuffles through a couple of outfits, chucking them across her room. "Not this one, not that one." She repeats.

When she is done and up and ready, she opens her door, tiptoeing out into the living room. Sarah is still on the couch.

Michelle smiles awkwardly. "How do I look?" She opens both arms.

Sarah follows her friend up and down with both eyes, unapologetically. "Well, you look different." She snorts, crossing both of her arms.

"Different in a good way?" Michelle bites her lip. "Just…different, I don't know. I didn't know that you wore makeup. Did you go through my make up bag?" She laughs.

"I'm sorry, I thought that I would try something different." Michelle turns a shade of red. Smoothing out the bottom of her dress.

"It doesn't matter. But, do you think that you'll run into him at breakfast or something." Sarah smirks.

"No!" Michelle replies, shaking her head. "I just thought I would do it for me."

Sarah shrugs her shoulders. "Whatever. By the way, you can keep the makeup bag; I don't care."

Michelle nearly stumbles on her words. "Well, thanks." She licks her lips.

Sarah gets up off the couch, pushing past her friend. "Let's go, princess, I'm starving."

Sarah had decided that the girls would go out for some coffee and pancakes.

Michelle sits behind the wheel with hands at ten and two. Sarah is in the passenger seat.

"I see you keep looking at your phone. You waiting for a call from your boyfriend." Sarah smirks.

Michelle blushes, shaking her head. "Brian is not my boyfriend." She replies, keeping her eyes on the road.

The car makes a turn, signaling left.

Michelle parks the car in front of a small diner.

On a Saturday morning, the diner is about half full. Various young students or weekend warriors sit around square wooden tables with a mug of coffee and plates of yellow egg and crispy brown bacon.

"Just a second," Michelle replies, repositioning the car mirror so that she could play with a bit of her hair.

Sarah sighs and opens the passenger door, stepping out onto the parking lot.

Michelle grabs the mirror and tilts it, so she can see Sarah walks towards the diner. Then she leans the mirror back.

In between the passenger seat and the driver's seat is a small purse. Michelle had dumped the contents of the makeup bag into her purse. She slings it around her shoulder and then steps out of the car.

The two girls find a table at the diner and take a seat.

A young waitress with large eyes and a nametag that reads, "Christie" takes their order.

She gives Sarah a one-two look over, pursing her lips. Then picks up the menus and heads back to the kitchen.

Michelle had ordered the Caesar salad with no dressing and an ice water. While Sarah had ordered a stack of pancakes.

When the plates arrive, Sarah helps herself to a large stack of pancakes by drizzling them in a thick coat of syrup and cream.

Michelle hears a giggle or two from another table. A group of young girls that are probably around nineteen or twenty.

One of them sees Michelle turn around and quickly covers her smirk. "Freak," She hears one of them mutter.

Michelle looks over at her bald friend with no eyebrows; with a handful of pancake mix on the table and a dribble of syrup that hangs from her chin like a stalactite in a cave.

Freak. Freaks. The voice rebounds in Michelle's earlobe and into her brain. The snickering has grown much louder now. Like pesky mosquitos stinging her neck.

"It was her," The voice in her head tells her. Sarah. The Freak.

She plays with her salad for a minute or two, piercing a tomato with the tip of her fork. The tomatoes red juicy guts ooze out from its side like an open sore.

Michelle continues to eat, nibbling at her plate. Would they ever stop? Freak.

"But I am the most beautiful woman in the room," She thought. But aren't I? The waitress comes back and refills their water glasses.

On the name tag is the word, "Ugly." Ugly. Michelle shakes her head. The table of girls is giggling again. The people on the street in front of the bar last night are here as well. She can feel it in her blood. Here to watch a couple of freaks.

"Is everything alright," The waitress fills up the glass. This shakes Michelle out of her daze. The name tag reads Christie again. Back too normal. Michelle nods her head.

The two continue to eat. Well, at least Sarah does. Slicing and dicing her pancakes.

Michelle's heart begins to drum. Was she going to be sick?

But here is the voice again.

"You are just as ugly as the nametag read," It replies. "Sarah wanted to be just like you. So, she changed her appearance, didn't she."? Didn't she.

Michelle grabs the side of her head. Got it hurt so bad.

She gets up from the table, digging into her purse for a small wad of cash. One foot in front of the other. Sarah looks up at her friend walk out of the diner.

Outside, in the parking lot, Michelle closes both of her eyes. Trying to breathe in the world through both nostrils and exhale out the bullshit.

The morning air is crisp and refreshing. The street is full with a patrol of cars and commuters, honking horns and impatient people.

"Is everything alright," Sarah whispers, coming after her. She stops about a foot or two away from her friend.

Michelle bites her tongue. "Michelle..." Sarah replies to her silence.

"What's...wrong with you!" Michelle snorts, stringing along a choppy sentence. Tears in the corner of her eyes.

"What?" Sarah replies. "You need help, I know what you did!" Michelle retorts, facing her friend.

"What...," Sarah says, taking a breath between syllables.

"You shaved your head, and you quit your job, Sarah." Michelle cries, unable to hold back a couple of sobs.

"Better now than never," Sarah spits, biting her lip.

"You're turning into something else. People are looking at you, wondering if you are insane. You don't see it. They think that I am like you. But I am beautiful, Sarah." Michelle yells.

"Since when does any of that matter, Michelle. What are you talking about!" Her friend replies, crossing both of her arms.

"You need to act normal again." Michelle hums. Shaking her head.

Sarah laughs to herself. "What is normal, Michelle. You think nobody else can tell that you did your hair or that you can barely stand up on those heels. Who are you supposed to be this morning? Who are you trying to impress!"

Michelle unzips her purse and dumps the materials onto the ground. A tube of lipstick rolls under her foot.

She flings the purse away. Breathing hard.

"I guess nobody now!" Michelle spurts, wiping away a tear from her eye. She stumbles a bit before picking herself up.

"Michelle!" Sarah grits, chasing after her friend.

Michelle walks alongside the sidewalk, leaving the parking lot behind. She wipes another tear away.

Michelle stops. "I'm not normal…you're the one who is telling me that I am not normal!"

At the intersection, the light turns green, and a station of motor vehicles take off down the road, chugging exhaust from their rusty pipes.

"Don't ever come near me again; I might catch something." Michelle begins to laugh, pointing the finger at Sarah. The finger wiggles in the air like a worm on the end of a hook.

"What is going on with you?" Sarah interrupts. "Take the car and drive until the tank is empty, you freak." Michelle throws her the car keys, landing at her feet.

"Michelle! Stop!" Sarah shrieks, picking up the keys. When the crosswalk sign lights up Michelle steps out onto the street.

With every footstep, the heels on her feet click together. She adjusts the heel on her foot. She takes it off, turns around, and flings it at Sarah on the sidewalk.

Sarah picks up the shoe, shaking her head. "Michelle!" She screams. Her friend barely has enough time to turn her head as the speeding truck rears through the red light, but not before hitting a road bump.

Michelle is hit by the truck at about fifty miles an hour, slightly faster than the appropriate limit, as one would be trying to make it through the yellow.

Tires screech, the driver throws up both hands, skidding off to one side. Michelle's body is sucked underneath the truck like a piece of lint on an apartment floor being picked up by a vacuum cleaner.

Then chewed up and spit out. Michelle's body cartwheels down the road like a bloody ragdoll, limb over a limb.

The driver of the truck sprints out into the street. Once one person begins to scream, another quickly joins in session. People pour out of the diner and local shops. Some on their knees and others trying to look away.

Sarah begins to join in on the seething mass, stumbling over to her friend. Michelle is on one side, breathing through a bloody hole in her throat.

The entire front side of her body is the color of charcoal and pavement. A lump of human grease in the middle of the road.

Remarkably, she manages to open both eyes, in and out of consciousness.

She sees Sarah through one eye. The other dangles down around her throat somewhere.

Michelle begins to take in one of her last breaths. For some reason unbeknownst to the universe, only a single thought runs through her head.

As the groups of people circle her, pale-faced and aghast. Come to see her.

"They have come to see me," She thinks. Before remembering something, she had said a long time ago.

Something she had told Sarah. But now that is in another lifetime. Michelle is dead before the thought is done.

"You are beautiful; and the luckiest woman in the world. Tell me, Sarah, what is it like for people to flock to you."

Bits and Pieces

Raising a set of kids is a tough business. Each parent must give a bit of themselves to the family. Sacrifices will be made, and people must remain strong. "It is my job to keep you fed and help you grow. Your father and I made an oath the day you were born. Now I have to finish it." Our mother liked to say.

She would also encourage us to be creative. My sister and I loved to play dress-up and other games, usually before supper. We would go through whatever we could find in the attic. But we were sneaky. Our mother never liked us creeping through dad's old stuff. Especially when I would put on a pair of his old shoes or his oversized pants that came down to my feet like a wet puddle on the floor.

Then I would look in the mirror. "I look just like him, huh." I smile and put my hands on both hips. "I see your father in the both of you. Bits and pieces." Our mother would wipe a tear from her eye.

Later, the three of us would sit around the dinner table with our hands together and our eyes closed. "What do you say, children," Mother whispers sweetly. "Thank you, father, for the bread and meat." We reply together.

When I open both of my eyes, my father is staring back at me. Just the head. The head is the color of lunchmeat, and the mouth is hung agape like an open sore.

"A family has to stick together. Your father keeps food on the table." Our mother retorts. She leans across the table and sticks a metal fork in father's cheek, using it as leverage to cut away a piece of the flesh with the knife in her other hand.

She plops apiece down onto each of our plates. I pick up my fork. "What is real love, my children." Mother gives us each a kiss. I just stare at the head.

"Sacrifice," My sister and I say together.

6:08 am:

The Morning After

(Poetry & Other Observations)

Sun and Moon

Someone once told me if the sun were a man then the moon is a woman, a young couple stuck in an unhappy marriage. The sun is loud and brash while the moon is bold and beautiful.

She is the life of the party and the topic of every conversation. The nightlife socialite. She stumbles into their bedroom half past six.

Her breath tastes of alcohol and her neck reeks of cologne, not her own. A pair of sunglasses rests on her face.

In the morning the sun is bitter. He is up for work, a leather briefcase in one hand a cup of coffee in the other. While the people of the world are asleep, lost in a river of denial.

In a short while, their day begins. He is to blame for what she did. Hangovers and hunched over faces commuting to work in silver automobiles. She tries to kiss his cheek he brushes her off.

His face red and flush with indignation. He's halfway out the door, one foot in front of the other. She begins to cry.

She couldn't dare tell him how alone she feels could she; up there by herself in the midnight hour.

Feeding the Monsters

My Thoughts On Writing

Why do we feel the need to bleed on the page? Writers. Sadomasochistic. Different words, same meaning. Although I'd like to imagine my life without the pen, I can't help but bleed red ink when I cut deep into my flesh. Or so I would imagine. I was born to do this, not to sound fanatical or ego driven. A statement that many like myself would agree too.

Although a few actually go all the way with it. I like to remind myself of the analogy of the murderer. You will find a few people in your life that you absolutely despise, although most people dream up fantastical ways for them to die they would never actually go through with it.

Were the monsters, writers; just like in the horror movies, we are those programmed to stick the knife in your back and twist. Writers are the individuals responsible for bringing our societies dirtiest and grimy revelations to the forefront. From the very dark corner and recesses of our minds. Writers show us who we really are.

Early on when I was a little boy, I too had found out I had this disease. My thoughts were pounding to get out and be heard. Like a ticking time bomb set to explode in six minutes and I was five and a half minutes past due.

This is during the early initial stages of this disease. Then someone hands you a pen, and the bomb goes off. At first, everything is a little messy. This can go on for years. Your words are hectic and uneven, but as others will soon discover; that unlike them, you are very sick. They will tell you the four most important words a writer can ever be told. If you are lucky. "There is something there." That's all a writer really needs is someone to tell them that what they are doing is worthwhile. After that, the rest is up to you to gain a wider audience and acceptance.

Although I do love writing, particularly stories about murderers, thieves, and maniacal villains. I write because I have to and have done so for most of my life. It gives me peace and slows down the mechanical wheel turning in my head that would otherwise tell me to go out and pillage, or burn down the neighbor's house and forget about this world for an hour or two. Some people drink, others smoke. I write.

To put it simply, for me this feeds the beast.

Angels & Demons

The two of us used to be in love, do you remember when.

We used to believe in the magic and beauty of the world.

I do, she tells me. But our battle is a war fought between the demon and angel on our shoulder.

One is holding a pink rose between its teeth, and the other rests its head on a thicket of thorn.

Both are prideful. Either believe that he is just as important.

One of them dreams of a scrupulous betrayal, and the other imagines a world together in harmony.

You and I are in the middle.

Cadavers

She has a look about her. Is it her cold blue lips or soft skin?

Like that of a corpse washed up on the beach. Reaching out for something.

She wanted to be loved. But all I did was use her. Mold her into what I thought fit best for us.

There is no Heaven. There are only two types of people you meet in Hell.

Those who tell a tale of lust and love or cry about betrayal and heartache.

.

Then There Were Two

Sometimes, I wish life would pick up the phone and tell me what this is all about.

I had driven everybody away. Except for her.

Her eyes were full of wonder, and my thoughts are eager.

We like asking each other simple questions.

Like, "Do you think somewhere in the universe, there are two people, just like us, who sit together on the grass and look up at the stars.

But, in their heads, are simultaneously plotting each other's murders?"

I Am in Need of an Enchantress

Tell me that you are real and that you are out there.

I am in need of the girl dressed in black, this gypsy woman. Her eyes are a color darker than her soul.

She is the type of girl to play with fire just to feel what it is like to get burned.

Because the hot orange flame couldn't hurt as much as the people in her past have hurt her.

{Love me tenderly or do not love me at all, she whispers in my ear.}

She is the woman of my dreams by the bottom of the glass. White lines on the table counter, white lies between our lips. Bitterness under my breath.

Searching for love like a needle prodding a dehydrated vein. Delirious in a post-teenage wasteland. Digging for a lifeline in the sand, sunburned and world-weary.

But wait,

She whispers in my ear as she mounts me, raising my flag, her eyes thick with lust and our love stronger than ever. "If a flower blooms in the desert, is it a miracle or act of God."

Daffodils

Don't cry over him, because he picked another girl over you.

He picks them by the handful, like daffodils.

His eyes are the same color as the black pit in his soul.

You were right to question him sooner than later. It was the best thing you ever did.

You untied your ropes and got out of there as quickly as you could, and didn't look back.

You refused to be another one of his victims.

The Earth is Flat and Long

If the earth really is flat and long, then why do I keep running back into you.

Somebody told me that blood is thicker than water, but my eyes are red and stained with tears.

I have come to believe that love is a game, but nobody has the rulebook and that the people who end up together are similar to children, making the rules up as we go along.

Observation #1

Life is a lot like a horror film.

You are playing the part of the director, and the lead role.

Surround yourself with a cast of characters that work for you.

Find someone who'll stick with you, through thick and thin. The dark and the cold and the lonely.

Someone who'll tell you that your idea sucks, or that the killer might not actually be dead.

Remember to say, thank you.

At the end of a film, if it is any good, the audience will stand up, and deliver a unanimous roar of applause. Most will turn towards the director, or the actor, and congratulate them.

Nobody ever sits there, quietly, as the credits roll across the screen, reading the hundreds of other names.

It takes an army to uplift a general. Remember that, if you are ever successful and look up at the stars and wonder how you got here.

Observation #2

Life is like committing a murder.

Some people can get away with it, and some people cannot.

Once you have developed a plan, stick with it.

But remember, success is in the details. Don't forget the little things.

Be sure to wipe the fingerprints and clean the gun.

Have a place to keep the bodies.

Write the Novel You've Always Wanted to Read.

Write the novel that you have always wanted to read.

That is the key.

Think back on childhood, and whatever English gibberish your teacher or parents forced you to inhale, toss it out the window.

Stop trying to be proper, or try and explain the theory of life with your writing. Stop it. Stop trying to write, *War & Peace*.

Remember the first bit of fiction that you picked up, and could not put back down. Flipping through pages, underneath the bed covers with your flashlight.

The novel that taught you, that reading could be fun.

Write that novel.

Bloody Pond

Being a horror writer is nothing to be ashamed of.

If somebody is offended by your work, they have obviously never gotten away with murder.

If they felt the rush that I feel, putting my bloody pen to paper. That would be enough.

In real life, you just have to put up with people.

In the fiction world, I select who lives and who dies.

I would rather be the big fish, swimming in a small bloody pond. That's life.

Questions and Answers

The Following are Questions sent in by readers like you.

If you would like your question answered or possibly featured in any upcoming work, you will find me at @afterdark_no_dreaming.

Let's get to reading.

1. When is scary too scary? - Alex.

- That is a great question. I do not think that you can ever get enough scares! My job is to dig down into your psyche and mess it up.

2. What is the most influential piece of horror writing still stuck in your mind today? – Bralyn

- Many different artists have influenced me for a variety of reasons.
- If we are just speaking horror, then Stephen King's "Night Shift" short story collection is probably it. I'd highly recommend it.

"The Ledge," "The Boogeyman," or "Quitters Inc." are some of my favorite stories from the book!

3. What is your thought process when writing? - Veoncee Collins

- Writing is, and will always be, therapeutic for me. When writing is at its best, you should only be focused on the story.
- A sort of Zen-like quality. You wanna feel like a couple of L.A. hipsters doing yoga together.

4. What inspired you to write these types of stories? - Anjali More

- I get this question a lot. I think I like writing psychological thrillers because I am obsessed with the reason people make the choices they make and do the things that they do.
- Most of my stories revolve around ordinary people who do extraordinary things.
- Haven't you ever looked at someone you're mad at and wanted to kill him or her? There is a reason for that. That's the real story, not the actual murder, but the motivation behind the killing.
- That's how a best seller is written.

5. If you live one day, have you lived one more day, or one less? - Matheus C.

- Hmm, why you trying to stump me with these tough questions! Well, I suppose it matters what you did that day. Right?

6. How long does it take you to come up with an idea? – Brianna

- Anywhere from a couple of hours to a couple of years. I have an idea for a novel I have been working on for five years now.

7. What motivates you to start writing? – Sreetma

- I can't explain it, but every artist has an urge to create. Rather you are a singer, dancer, painter, or horror writer. I just naturally like writing stories; it is how I express what is going on in my head.

8. Are you a fan of scary movies? - Rida

- Yes, of course. But I like smart, scary movies. Ones with a unique perspective and movies that have something to say. But every now and then I'll watch a trashy horror film. My guilty pleasure is Friday the 13th Part V. It's so bad it's a great film. It was made in the mid 80's, and I'm pretty sure the entire cast and crew were on cocaine. Somebody had to have been on drugs to okay the finished product.

9. How do you deal with writer's block? - Graciela Shelly

- Read a book by a writer you've never read, watch a movie you've never seen, or listen to a new musician. Just dive into somebody else's world for an hour or two and soak up some ideas. Everybody has an interesting viewpoint of the world if you sit down and talk to him or her. Remember that.

10. What inspires your dark humor? - Radhika Sethi

- Probably my parents. My father has always had a great sense of humor. I translate that into my scary stories.

11. What made you start writing- Grayden Dunham

- My love for books. I wanted to see if I could write my own stories.

12. How did you start writing? - Emma

- I wrote on and off growing up as a kid, but I didn't really get into it until I took a creative writing class in the 12th grade. Encouragement is big, and I have been lucky enough to have a couple of key players in my life to tell me to keep going at it.

> 13. What do you do when you cannot think of a single story? - Maria Soumela Christou

- Go do something else. Go work out or go read a book. Just let your mind relax for a second.

> 14. Will you ever write another genre other than horror? - Fatima Nafeed

- I don't know. I have always wanted to tackle an Agatha Christie type murder mystery. But who knows, really. Life is kind of crazy like that. I think it might even be fun and write a romance book under a different name or something.

> 15. How long in total did it take to write this book? - Bobby

- Well, I have been writing these stories for about a year. So, 12 months in total.

> 16. What If you woke up and found yourself living in one of your stories? What would you do? - Pratik Pathare

- Write myself a new ending and get the HELL out of there. You guys know how twisted I am.

17. What's your favorite writing spot? - Eleanor Harper

- Anyplace that is quiet with no barking dogs or traffic noises or people coming up to me and asking for my autograph. Just kidding. I'm not that cool.

18. How do you get the right setting without repeating it in other stories?

- I just remember what type of stories I have written. But, every writer must have a niche. If somebody picks up one of my books, they know that a substantial portion of my stories is set in suburbia. I grew up in a small town and know that setting very well so I can bring that culture to life in my stories.

19. Who are your favorite authors? - Robert B.

- Ray Bradbury, Stephen King, Rod Sterling, R.L Stine, Scott Smith, and Agatha Christie.

20. What Advice do you give to writers who don't know what to write about? - Katie.

- Write about what you know. Period. If you are just a kid, then write about your experiences in school. You don't need a ton of "life experiences" to be a great writer. Because you already have your own. Nobody else's life on this planet is 100 percent like your own. Everybody has a unique perspective.

   21. When you were a kid, did you see yourself ever writing a book? - Bree Dossey

- Yes. I think I tried to write a book when I was 10 or 11 but lost the floppy disk I had saved my work on. (Yes kids, I am old. I said floppy disk)

   22. If you were able to change one thing in the world. What would it be? – Wiktoria

- That traveling the world was a requirement for young people. It really alters your perception of life and people when you visit other places.
- Everybody on the planet wants similar things out of life. The biggest lie told is that we are different because we live on one side of the rock than another person.

   23. Who are your influences? - Crystal J.

- People for different reasons influence me. Ray Bradbury and his writing style, Stephen King and his genius ideas, Agatha Christie for her characters, Scott Smith for his plotting, and Rod Sterling and R.L Stine for building a media empire.
- I am also heavily influenced by music and art. Anything Pink Floyd did in the 70's; Ziggy Stardust and the Spiders from Mars by David

Bowie is a big album for me or a singer-songwriter by the name of Nick Drake and his work way back when.

- As far as more modern music, Glass Animals album Zabba is probably my favorite record of the last ten years; I also like earlier Kanye West, and Eminem back when he was actually good.

About the Author

Kyler currently lives in Los Angeles, California.

For more information on his work, please visit @afterdark_no_dreaming on Instagram.

He may also be reached by email at afterdarknodreaming@gmail.com